Olio

Queen Anne's Lace Publishing

Foreword

The Massillon Public Library Adult Writer's Group was established in February of 2023. It was only supposed to last the month of February, to help kick start writers' passion and to kick off the *Your Novel is Now* multi-month program at the library.

However, the writing group was such a success that it lasted far beyond February.
In February 2024, they deemed themselves "Writers of the Round Table."

Many of the writers have since released books, and grown far beyond any of them dreamed.
The group meets twice a month, and has supported authors with editing, formatting, proofreading, and, most importantly, encouragement.

Contents

OUR WORLD   1

1. The Wilsons   2

2. First Time   9

3. The Summer of the Pink Slip   15

4. Super Daisy, My Hero   25

5. Dream Home   31

6. The Bed   34

7. The Throw-Away People   37

OTHER WORLDS   41

8. Adelaide, The Bookbinder   43

9. The Orphaned Twins   51

10. A "Real" Golf Story   55

KINDLING   60

11. Fire Flight   61

12. AfterFlare: Mike Harden's Journal   84

TOGETHERNESS   110

13. 2AM Call   111

14. He Saved Her   114

15. The Proposal   117

THE UNKNOWN   123

16. A Quiet Dance   124

17. BloodRose   126

18. The Search for Lake Atagahi   147

THE FAITH   159

19. The Centurion   160

20. The Bloody Man   167

21. The Tale of the Country Cat   173

22. The Fable of the Christmas Spider   190

About the Authors   198

OUR WORLD

Stories that take place in our world. First times, favorite pets, our darkest struggles, and our highest dreams.

The Wilsons by V. Aglow

First Time by Dwight Parrish

Super Daisy, My Hero by Donna J. Bunner

Dream Home by Jana Day

The Throw-Away People by IMA Live

The Bed by MKS Cooper

The Wilsons

V. Aglow

HERE COMES THE WILSONS: never late, always on time.

Everyone knows there's two days a week you want to see the Wilsons: Sunday and Monday. On the corner of South Smith St. and Hillsbur, the two of them open the double doors together. The doors are made of Ironwood known, as *Oleaceac* in Africa, making it wide and heavy.

Mr. and Mrs. Wilson's morning routine consists of turning on the lights and taking out the stick out of the windows. They unlock the exit door, and the side doors, which have longer sticks for extra security.

Mrs. Wilson lifts the fabric shades off the windows and continues her routine. She goes into the kitchen and turns on the stove by lighting a match. A *whoop* sounds happens and the fire appears.

On the other side of the diner, where most customers go, Mr. Wilson assures that the icebox is still working. He recounts the beverages to serve the customers at their request. Then he leads on to fill bowls with pizzles and beer nuts and places them alone the custom-made, one-of-a-kind bar, made out of the same Ironwood the door is made of.

Mrs. Wilson has already prepared and set aside her well known apple butter, steaming hot dinner rolls, and spiced cracker appetizers. The locals' favorites, cornbread and chili and the wiggle-your-toes salad with a series of salad dressings; Grapefruit Citrus, French Hot & Spice , and Watermelon Blast are all prepared. Along with other café meals, the locals keep coming back after all these years. There's one ingredient that stands out over others diners, yet they can't seem to figure it out.

Customers often asked "WHAT'S YOUR SECRET?"

Mrs. Wilson looks them straight in there eyes, gives them this big smile and raises her eyebrows and — walks away.

It isn't long after setting up and readying themselves for the first customers, the first two regulars come in and sit in there usual spots at the bar. They talk about the latest hot topic in the newspaper.

A few minutes later Ellen and Betty come in and sit near the window closet to the back. Both are well know around town. Ellen is active in the community. She helps with fundraisers to help the community and churches by feeding and clothing the less fortunate. And as for Betty, everyone knows that Betty owns a small hair salon. If you want to be the center of attention at proms, holidays, or special events, she's your way to go. If you want to be the center of attention at the end of life, she can do that too. Yes, she's a corpse hairdresser as well.

Betty's hair salon is the place to go. Just Saying.

When they're not as busy, Ellen and Betty meet every week, usually around the same time on Tuesday.

I'm sure their are conversations mostly about what they do from week to week, the people they encounter, a ton of gossip, and all around just catching up.

It's around 1:30PM and the diner is half full.

Looks like Mr. Fox decided to stop by the diner today.

Oops, I guess not, hmm I was sure... Okay, he slowed down enough, so... That was interesting. He drove right along.

Now who is that? I'm not sure if I've seen him before. Oh wait, that's Old Man Sleepy.

What is he doing riding that bike? He's a mechanic. What's that all about? We'll find out soon enough.

It isn't long before the diner was at its full capacity. It's now 3:30 PM and the crowd starts to dwindle down. There's one customer at the bar. He seems to be going through a lot. Mr. Wilson goes to him.

Mrs. Wilson has found her way back into the kitchen doing what she does to stay ready to serve customers as they come in.

Well, well, well- to no surprise Squirrel has found his way back into the town. He lives way down the other side of the railroad tracks. No one really knows where exactly he lives. You can hear him a ways off. He's no stranger- everyone loves him. He greets everyone with this smile and dimples as wide as a dime. He's got no front teeth and his hair is cold, black and curly.

Before he gets inside the diner door he meets Mr. Wilson. You can hear him saying, "Whatchu got! Whatchu got!"

Mr. Wilson replies saying, "Same ol'. Same ol'."

Squirrel's laugh sounds like he needs to cough. He heads over and takes a seat. Mr. Wilson comes over and starts talking about hunting season coming up. Since the diner closes at 7 PM,Mr. and Mrs. Wilson are coming down to the final two hours. It's now 5PM.

The Wilsons prepare for the last crowd of customers.

Okay, that's my queue. The fabric shades come down and the lights are out. The Wilson's are closing for the day. The sound of the concrete factory on the next street over, near the railroad track, is done for the day as well. The occasional bikers and walkers come, trying to get to the other side of the town before the last train comes through.

The street lights are own. Hollison St. is dark without the street lights. It would be unsafe to walk alone that side of Hillsbur. You can fill in the blank.

This next morning the Wilson's receive their truck delivery around 9AM. They are set and ready. Peter, the delivery guy backs up towards the side door and off comes the supplies. It doesn't take long for Mr. Wilson and Peter to begin a small talk and cracking jokes. Mrs. Wilson wastes no time in putting all of the supplies away.

The hour comes and they are ready to serve.

They are never late, always on time.

Today's special is called 'Three Sister's Stew.' labeled as number three on the menu, served with blueberry pie. It's sure to be the top order of the day.

Judge Anthony stops by for lunch. We rarely see him, with all the issues going on with the Dubock Twins Boy's.

They are keeping the town buzzing with chatter. It's been said that the Dubocks Twins went and married the Walker sisters without their father's permission. Now you would have to know who their father is. Everyone knows the Walker family! Though his family calls him Daddy, we know him as Preacher Walker. Preacher Walker is 6ft 7 man with lumberjack hands, arms like Popeye's and a deep voice.

The Walker family has 12 children and they live on a country road borderline between two states: Arkansas & Louisana. Since it's Friday, it is not unusual that most of the town is out somewhere exciting, such as the *Cat's* football game or the Country Line Dance Hall. And, of course, the town's rebel teens are hanging out at the car wash.

Saturdays are typical, hold the exception of the time year when Mrs. Wilson receives a bouquet of flowers. Even the regulars keep this day in mind. Shortly after opening the doors, Mr. and Mrs. Wilson embrace one another as they go about their normal routine.

Mrs. Wilson's sisters were traveling midwives who care for town residents as well. Mrs. Wilson had two sisters, Sadi and Annah. The sisters grew up in Tennessee and lived in poverty with an influenced background.

Their father spent time away as a traveling salesman. As for their mother, she was a teacher and a nurse who cared for town. Mrs. Wilson and her two sisters moved to Arkansas when they were young. Sadi was the oldest, Annah was the youngest, and then there was Mrs. Wilson. After both their parents passed away, they were left to care for themselves.

They grew older and made their lives comfortable. Daisy and Sadie were midwives, and even though they had no children of their own, they had a passion for the profession. They traveled to a nearby town helping deliver mothers in labor. But one time, there was a fire and Daisy and Sadie never came back home.

The bouquet of flowers is for them.

My name is Hazel. I love on South Smith and Hillsborough Street. My porch is high and angled towards the Wilsons. Right now I am sitting on the porch swing, writing everything I see with my own eyes and the journal left behind by Mrs. Wilson at the sister's address: South Smith St.

First Time

Dwight Parrish

AND JUST LIKE THAT... it was over!

   She begged for more.

   Her body craving his energy.

   Her soul feeling his passion.

   Her heart hoping he would stay.

It was obvious tonight would be different. Shawn's breath blew in and out rapidly. His left hand searched for the left turn signal, as if it was not where he left it. Shawn followed the vehicle ahead of him into the cramped parking lot that revealed more cracks and turns than cars. Before he knew it, he had maneuvered his way back out onto the street and had to re-enter the lot. Once he saw a parking spot, he began to make his move.

Backward. Forward. Backward. Forward. Backward.

His vehicle finally rested at odds with the parallel lines.

After turning off the engine, Shawn pulled down his sun visor, then flipped it back up. He lifted up his console and closed it. He slowly reached in his glove box and came out empty handed. But the driver ahead of him was still standing nearby, smoking a cigarette. Shawn picked up his cell phone and studied his wallpaper photo with the time and date stamp. Finally! The long smoker flicked away the cigarette and entered a door, three doors away from where Shawn parked.

It was a nondescript building that sat dangerously close to a bundle of railroad tracks. No visible sign. Not exactly what Shawn had envisioned. He actually passed by this building quite frequently on his way downtown. It used to be a train station back in the day and he had always wanted to ride the train.

As a child, Shawn would imagine what was taking place inside:

A solider, with an army-green duffle bag, sitting on a hard bench. Deep in thought, wondering what boot camp would be like and if he would make it back home. In the back of the room would be a single mother with two small kids. They were shouting from the old vending machine as the loud speaker crackled "*Now boarding for St. Louis.*"

At least that's what he saw on television.

Shawn checked his appearance in his rearview mirror and exited the car. He retraced the steps of the smoker and opened the glass door to walk inside. The mood lighting greeted him first. Red, sexy musical notes danced on all four walls in perfect rhythm with the jazz sounds filling the space.

She was sitting just inside the door. Her smile was sexier than the notes on the wall, which had now reversed their movement around the room. She had flawless, caramel cheeks that displayed a hint of red blush. She spoke the language of a poet.

"Hi... Welcome to *Blue Notes*!" greeted the Hostess.

"Hi!" Shawn responded. How much is it?"

"It depends on what you want to do," she said.

The woman handed him a menu of options which he quickly reviewed and paid with cash. Shawn hurriedly walked away. Not another word. He spotted a small, make-shift bar across the room and headed in that direction. He ordered a glass of merlot and found a small table in the back of the room.

Shawn was heading into his senior year at TSU and feeling self-conscious. He frequently glanced over at the hostess and wondered if she recognized him. Would she tell anyone? Was she laughing on the inside? He last saw her at the end of spring semester, when she gave her final lecture to his class of about two-hundred students. He took a long sip of wine, hoping to mellow out his anxiety and raise his confidence.

As Shawn scanned the room, he noticed a gentleman walking towards him with the swagger of a brother on the streets of Harlem.

"What's up, man! My name is Reign and I'm the Host. Welcome to *Blue Notes*!"

Shawn stood and extended his right hand, placing his left arm around Reign's shoulder, reining him in for a brief man hug.

"What's up bruh... I'm Shawn," he responded.

"We're all about networking here. I appreciate you stopping through. I see that you made your selection. I just need you to write your name down in the order you wish to go," Reign said.

Reign handed Shawn a blank sheet of paper that was numbered from 1-10. Shawn wrote his name down in the third spot just to keep from going first. *Shawn Washington.*

"Now you know, everyone else is going to place their name after you, right? But don't worry, I got you. This is your first time."

"Appreciate it!"

"What alias do you go by?" Reign asked.

Shawn was caught off guard and didn't know what else to say, so he said, "Shawn Washington."

Once again, they shared a quick, brotherly hug and Reign swaggered his way back through the red, sexy notes.

Men and women were affectionately greeting each other with warm hugs and Shawn's anticipation began to rise as he tipped his wine glass more frequently. He was starting to feel as if he and the music were one.

"Shawn Washington!" The loudspeaker called.

It was at that moment that Shawn wished he would have provided an alias. If his college professor didn't recognize his face, his name might jolt her memory. Feeling relaxed and confident, Shawn stood up and followed Reign's lead. It was show time!

Just like that…it was over!

"More… more!"

"Don't stop now!"

"I know you got more in you." The red-haired woman was begging at this point. "Why are you leaving?"

"Thank you so much!" Shawn calmly said.

And with that, he turned and walked away with a swagger of his own. He had knocked it out of the park his first time at bat. He was no longer a virgin.

He was a Spoken Word Artist performing live on stage.

The Summer of the Pink Slip

Okema N. Bassett

It began like any other work day, hurried, with a cross between an inspirational speaker and *Pitbull* playing in my car.

Once stopped at a light, I applied lip gloss. The commute was short, but impactful. After arriving downtown at my job, I jumped out of the car inspired and energized. I unlocked the front door, punched in the code for the alarm and walked over to start the coffee machine. The day was off to a great start!

I was the first employee there, as I'd arrived thirty minutes prior to the start time of 9AM. It's always cool to cruise into the day before the phones were ringing off the hook and the emails began to dominate my inbox. It was warm outside as the sun shone through the east-facing windows. We were on the cusp of summer, and we were only a couple of weeks from Memorial Day. I enjoyed the peace of being in the office alone and the feeling of accomplishment as I read and responded to the emails from the previous evening.

Employees began arriving around 8:55Am. They said, "Good morning," and proceeded to their desks.

I responded with a jovial, "Good morning," and continued working.

Strangely enough, Karen K. Kunningham, Regional Manager, arrived around 9:15AM to the office. The strange thing about it is she is employed by the same company as myself, but she worked in Cleveland. There was no mention of her being in our office on the office calendar, so it was definitely an odd occurrence. Karen, dressed in a white suit, walked over to the *Keurig* machine and made a cup of what smelled like French vanilla coffee. She greeted the employees nearest the front door, then she asked me if she could speak with me for a moment in the conference room.

I agreed, but not before I noticed the toilet paper on the bottom of her shoe. It felt just as odd as her being there unannounced. We both walked towards the conference room and sat opposite one another. Karen had a folder with my name on it sitting on the table. She stated that business had been slower than usual and all the normal verbiage that is said when you're being laid off.

At some point, she handed me documentation to sign, along with the folder that displayed my name. The walk back to my desk was filled with many thoughts. *What's next? Thank God I have an emergency fund stashed.* And many other things.

I quickly boxed my possessions, took them to my car, texted my co-workers of what had occurred. I received several messages of how sorry they were and other messages that I expected never came. The relationships built with your co-workers are complex. Some of the relationships are built on true friendship and others are merely built on convenience, once the convenience of seeing one another daily has been removed, so has the "friendship".

My first call was to my boyfriend Graham. We'd been together for one and a half years. We lived in different cities, 94 miles apart, however we were fervently devoted to one another. Graham initially thought I was joking when I stated I had been released from my position, as he recalled my dedication to the company. He reassured me that we're in this together and for me not to worry. I heard the concern in his voice. These are the moments when long-distance relationships are tough, and I wished he were there to comfort me.

As I drove away from my downtown job of 10 years, I thought deeply about my next career move, my next move overall and what to do with the remainder of the day. As I placed my sunglasses on, I was reminded of the beauty of the day. I drove to the nearest city park, parked my pearl white luxury sedan and admired the landscape that boasted massive spring blooms of tulips, daffodils and purple hyacinth. I was also reminded by the beauty of the flowers that all things bloom in their season. I sat on the warm metal bench, slid off my peep-toe, navy pumps and took in the scent and beauty of late spring; thinking how unfair life could sometimes seem. I silently said the "Serenity Prayer" in my head, hoping it would bring some sense of order to my racing thoughts.

It did.

JUNE

After getting a grasp on my new normal, I applied for unemployment and the checks were substantial enough to sustain my monthly mortgage payments, along with my household bills.

Thank God!

After raising a family and working since my teenage years, I thought this might be the well-deserved break I'd needed. For decades I'd been dashing from one child's event to the next... parent teacher conferences, football games, volleyball games, award ceremonies. A break was in order! My main priorities were finding a new position, spending time with my beloved family and also cultivating the romance myself and Graham had started in 2021. Since I could electronically report to the unemployment office, I split my time between Franklin, Ohio and Landers, Ohio.

Summer was in full swing boasting sunny days filled with blues skies and endless possibilities. Graham worked second shift at a manufacturing plant in the city in which he resided. We adored one another and found creative ways to spend valuable time together. With Graham working on the weekdays we usually waited until the weekends to go on dates.

Date nights or days are always a delight. Sometimes planned, usually spontaneous, always fun!

Our first date was a picnic under a red maple tree in a nearby park. The temperature was in the high 70s, with a slight breeze. It was late afternoon. Our wicker picnic basket stored a small pre-made charcuterie board, antipasto salad, grapes, strawberries, *Riesling* wine, silverware, cloth napkins and two small wine glasses. Graham retrieved the red and white checkered picnic blanket from the car trunk. We selected the perfect spot under the tree and Graham spread the throw over the plush, green grass. We sat our picnic basket down, got settled on the blanket, turned on smooth jazz and noshed on the delicious fare.

The simplicity of our bond is astonishing even to us. We first fell for one another as teenagers at Landers Middle

School. Our crush was evident. It was written all over our faces.

My strict upbringing and laborious schedule would keep me preoccupied with religious and academic pursuits.

One day as we were walking after track practice, we found ourselves in a secluded parking lot. Amazingly enough, finally after days, weeks and months of subtle flirting, we shared the most sensational, sensual and luscious kiss. His lips were full, his skin the shade of cocoa, his grip strong. I desired him and I could tell he desired me. As fate would have it, one kiss would be all that we'd share during the year of 1989. Our home lives would separate us, as we both moved on the same day... the last day of school.

Unbeknownst to our middle school selves, we wouldn't see one another again for 32 years.

Social media would be the vehicle that brought us back together. A direct message (DM) from Graham started it all. We both were in a place in our lives that life had chewed us up and spit us out! A true friendship is just what the doctor ordered! We began corresponding on social media and then graduated to texting, then talking on the phone. Our friendship was refreshing, yet nostalgic. We spent our time filling in the blanks for the last three decades. There were stories from childhood, relationship conversations and simply therapeutic banter.

I looked forward to our beautiful exchange daily.

I'd go home to Franklin, Ohio from Monday morning to Thursday afternoon, making sure I'd shop for food, household goods, *really* clean the upstairs bathrooms and just catch up with everyone and make sure all were thriving. We exchanged calls and texts while I was spending time in Landers, but spending quality time is a necessity. I'd usually cook a homemade meal or pick up carry out that we enjoyed so we could break bread together. I love the unique individuals that are my family. I have amazing friends in Franklin, all different but all great in their own right.

Commuting back and forth was refreshing. I varied between listening to many genres of music, spiritual sermons and insightful podcasts. This was a time that I could use selfishly. Periodically, I'd call family members and friends to catch up.

Arriving in Landers, Graham would be waiting for me on the apartment stoop. I'd provide him with my GPS information as I pulled out of the driveway. We both felt secure, knowing the GPS allowed him to track my arrival and me to know should anything go wrong, he'd be aware of it right away. I always looked forward to turning that corner and seeing his handsome face and stunning smile!

I jumped out of the car and we shared an embrace and luscious kiss!

Thursday evening, I arrived at the apartment home around sevenish. To my surprise, Graham had gotten off of work early and started a bonfire.

We loved the warmth of the fire, intermingled with the cool of the evening, set under the small grove of trees in the backyard.

Over a glass of red wine, for me, and a glass of whiskey on the rocks, for him, we shared our week and gazed at one another over the flame of our fire. Who knew that this small, Midwest town that we'd met in so long ago would be the very same town that would bring us back together and nurture our love? Not us! We'd enjoy our intimate evening together with our bonfire blazing as well as our desire for one another. We'd awaken the next morning in Graham's room. I could see out of the bedroom window that the fire was still smoldering.

Our morning routine included one of us making coffee, reading together and going for an early walk, in an effort to stay active. It was blissful and a beautiful way to ease into the demanding day. Graham reported to work mid-day so we made the best of our mornings.

One particular Friday, after he reported to work, I decided to check out the local library to kill time. I noticed that there was a writing group starting the next week and I hoped to join. I wandered around the library, leafing through cookbooks, gardening books and ultimately heading back to Graham's place.

As I neared his place I saw Memphis, Graham's younger brother, who lived on the same street. We exchanged a wave as I slowly drove by.

JULY

As Saturday approached, I researched our next adventure: Edgewater Beach. It was only an hour drive from Landers.

On Saturday morning, we began the morning with our normal ritual of coffee and reading, but nixed our morning walk.

We prepared for the day, filled a cooler with bottled waters and cool drinks, grabbed our swimwear and beach towels and hit the road. As Graham drove, we found a radio station with smooth jazz and we drifted into a calming mental space. The ride was a breeze.

I relaxed in the passenger's seat and in no time we arrived at the beach. It was a sunny day with blue skies. And although there were many people present, it often felt like we were in our own movie and we were the leading characters. We quickly went to the public restrooms and changed into our swim gear. Once dressed we met in front of the restrooms, placed our clothes in a beach bag, spread the beach towels out and walked hand and hand to the edge of the water. It washed over our feet.

Ironically enough, we were at the beach in beach gear, but neither of us could swim. Swimming remains on our "bucket list" of things we plan to do.

Being unable to swim didn't hamper our joy. We basked in the sun, enjoying one another's company. We grabbed hot dogs from the concession stand nearby and enjoyed them with the drinks that we had in our cooler.

I lied on my beach towel relaxed and warm with sunglasses on thinking of many things. My thoughts wandered to how sometimes life will give you a curveball and what we must do to combat throwing in the towel.

Like when I received that pink slip I wasn't sure how my story would end, but the summer had been remarkable-courtesy of that pink slip!

Super Daisy, My Hero

Donna J. Bunner

Daisy had enough of Melanie snoring and jumped on top of the bundle on the bed. "What? What? Huh?" Melanie grunted, awakened abruptly. "Daisy, can't you let me sleep in? I don't have to get up early today," Melanie groaned as she rolled over to go back to sleep.

Daisy immediately jumped up on Melanie again and started kneading her paws on Melanie's hip.

Melanie's mom, Stephanie walked into her room and turned on her light. "Rise and shine, Mel. Time for breakfast. Oh look, Daisy is helping me with breakfast by buttering the biscuits with butter and strawberry jelly. Better yet, mastering her skills at piano playing. Multi-talented cat for sure."

Melanie sat up on her bed and began petting Daisy. "She's is still my best biscuit maker ever," said Melanie. She picked up Daisy and was glad she had Daisy to help her get through her tough classes this semester. That week, especially, with exams. Melanie had worked on her English term paper on Shakespeare until three in the morning. Daisy never left Melanie's side. She even followed Melanie into the bathroom, as if to comfort her if she needed it.

"Well, hup to it dear. We have your doctor appointment with the new asthma and allergy doctor at 10, and it will take us 45 minutes to get there," her mom said.

"Okay... I hate doctors- especially ones I don't know."

"I know sweetie. This guy was recommended by Jessie at church, so I hope that eases your mind some. Jessie said he really helped her allergies. He uses homeopathic products to start with."

"Okay Mom. I'll get dressed and be right down." Before Melanie stood up, she started petting Daisy. Daisy perched up and started rubbing against Melanie. Stroking her fur, she said, "I love my black and white snookems so much. Yes, Mommy does. You're my pretty girl. Yes you are."

Melanie got dressed and headed downstairs to breakfast. Mom had made her favorite- eggs and ham along with some wheat toast and orange juice. As Stephanie and Melanie ate, they talked about Melanie's exams. She got an A in Accounting I and an A- in German. Melanie was hoping to get an A on her paper she just finished, and she was sure she would make the Dean's List again. Two more semesters and she would be finished with her Bachelor's degree in Accounting. Then she would study for the CPA exam. Melanie always loved figures and numbers. She hoped one day to have her own small business and work from home doing bookkeeping and taxes.

Stephanie looked up at the clock and said, "Time to go Mel."

At the allergy/asthma doctor's office, Dr. Gregg was very nice and very thorough in asking questions. He asked Melanie how long has she had trouble with her sinuses and how long she had used her CPAP machine. He then ordered a chest x-ray and CT scan of the sinuses to see if his assumption was right.

"Okay, Melanie," he said, looking at the results. "We looked at your CT scan and chest x-ray. Your chest x-ray looks good. Your CT scan showed that your sinuses aren't draining properly and are clogging the vessels in your nose. We also saw two nasal polyps that are very small. I would recommend removing those, and do a balloon sinus dilation where we place a balloon in your sinus cavity to aid in draining the sinuses continually. "We also looked over your previous sleep study, and you stopped breathing 40 times during the study. Do you wear a CPAP at night?"

"Boy is that an issue," Stephanie said. "I keep telling her to put it on and wear it, but she won't."

"Mom, you know I hate that thing."

"I know. I know," said Stephanie.

"It's very important that you do wear it. It could throw your heart onto atrial fibrillation. Is it uncomfortable? We can try a different mask," Dr. Gregg interjected.

"It just has been hard to get used to. I'll try to do better," Melanie said.

"Good to hear."

"Hey, Doc... is it okay if I think about the surgery before I agree to it?" Melanie asked hesitantly.

"Absolutely. Please do. I know it's a lot to think about. I you have any questions, please don't hesitate to ask." Dr. Gregg stepped out of the room and Melanie and Stephanie headed for home.

"Melanie, time for dinner," Stephanie yelled up the steps.

Melanie was studying for her last final exam. There sat Daisy, right by Melanie's side.

"Be right down Mom!" Melanie yelled back.

During dinner, Melanie and Stephanie talked about the

surgery. Melanie said, "Mom, I think I thought of something."

"What's that dear?"

"Well, I was wondering why Daisy kept jumping on me in the middle of the night waking me up. I would wake up and pet her, and a couple of hours later she would jump on me again."

"She is definitely your cat, for sure. She's always been attached to you."

"Mom, I think I just put two and two together."

"What do you mean dear?"

"Well, I was thinking about how the doctor said I quit breathing in the middle of the night a lot of times. Forty, I think he said. Well, I think Daisy was saving my life by waking me up! She noticed I stopped breathing and came over to wake me up by nudging me and jumping on me, and when I didn't wake up she would 'play piano' on my chest until I woke up."

"You know, I think you're right. She will be as good as Liberace someday- as much as she plays on top of you," Stephanie said, laughing.

"I know, right?" Melanie chuckled.

"Well I agree. I think God used Daisy to help you, as well as leading us in the direction of sinus surgery. What are your thoughts?"

"I totally am fine getting the surgery. Whatever it takes to be able to breathe normally, I'm all for it."

After dinner, Melanie was hopeful that she would pass her exams with flying colors and would call the doctor's office to schedule the needed surgery. As for Daisy, she continued to be Melanie's black and white fluffy baby who was always by her side- and remained her superhero during the night.

Dream Home

Jana Day

I NEVER CONSIDERED OWNING a house until I married my husband, an architect. He believed his life would not be complete until he lived in a dwelling of his own design; created from his imagination and determination.

So far, we have settled for something in the middle, buying someone else's dream, wrecking it, and imposing our will. These homes we create are beautiful, but not the dream of either one of us. These reconstructed residences become the dreams of others.

My friends often comment that they could not imagine expending so much time and energy to create such a masterpiece only to sell it. There is no emotional investment on our part only labor and materials. It's simple we do it to make money, to get one step closer to the dream because dreams, at least his dream, is not cheap.

Our date nights consist of dinner at a restaurant, with him drawing yet another version of our future home on paper napkins. He draws, I critique.

"What about a laundry room? I don't see one in the drawings. Can it be near the master bedroom?"

"Yes, but just focus on the concept." He says and hangs his head in defeat.

His frustration shows at my inability to look past the lines and see his vision. It's just that laundry has been on my mind since I have been hauling the clothes to the laundromat for the last two months, waiting for the plumbing to be completed, so the washer and dryer can be installed.

Renovations take longer when we both have demanding full-time jobs.

I want to have evenings and weekends free. The worries of lawn care and broken hot water heaters to be some else's concern. I want date nights to be filled with talk of trips and adventures, instead of plans that require me to work. Our weeknights spent sharing a bottle of wine over a leisurely dinner or watching mindless television without the guilt that we should be painting or installing baseboard. I want to stay in bed and make love on a rainy Saturday morning and not have one chore on our 'to do' list.

Instead, my Saturday mornings are likely to sound like this:

"Can you be ready to go in twenty minutes? Home Depot will be open and we need to place the order for the kitchen cabinets and pick out the countertop today."

"Can't you go without me? I would love to read the paper and have another cup of coffee."

"What if you don't like what I pick out? I can wait for you. Would thirty minutes be enough?"

I lay down the newspaper, gulp the last of my coffee, pull on my jeans then grab a scrunchie to contain my hair.

We drive to the big box store and choose the solid wood hickory cabinets and granite countertops. In six weeks, we'll install the cupboards ourselves. We choose the tile for the back splash and the grout then the garbage disposal and goose-neck faucet before heading back to scrape the last of the popcorn ceilings.

We ride in silence along the city streets passing lots, houses and apartments buildings, detouring so he can once again look at a vacant piece of land which he hopes may one day be the location of his dream. The one created from his imagination and determination.

I look at the apartment buildings and dream of renting.

The Bed

MKS Cooper

HE TRUDGES ALONG THE littered sidewalk that borders the busy street, waiting for an opening in the evening traffic. His arms are filled with what he has salvaged from the dumpsters and curbside detritus cast off by people he will never meet, who live a life substantially more blessed than his has been so far. He hopes their throwaways will provide him with some measure of warmth against the cold February night in downtown Chicago.

Four car lengths back the traffic slows almost to a stop and he scurries across the dirty, snow-edged pavement to the narrow strip of concrete that divides two lanes of highway, one going north and the other going south. The vehicles carry people who might as well be from another planet as far as he is concerned, for in his mind he doesn't belong to the same world they live in.

He talks to beings who can't be seen by anyone but him and listens as they talk back to him only, imaginary beings born in the world that he has created in his booze-infused brain, or what is left of it after the alcohol and delirium took over.

He places the dirty, worn blankets on the lane divider, a strip of concrete not much wider than two of those cots they give you to sleep on in the shelter he used to go to. He doesn't go there anymore because of the bugs and the smell of unwashed men and the screams in the night that keep a person awake.

Ignoring the honking horns that caution him otherwise, he spreads out his bounty of filthy, worn-thin blankets and discarded newspapers and sinks into his bed. Ready for sleep, he hopes the bad dreams will stay away; hopes the cop on this beat will stay away.

Lying on his back on the damp, cold surface, holding onto the side of the cement divider, trying to keep from rolling off into the traffic, he closes his eyes, seeking sleep, and smiles while listening to his long-dead mother lullaby him softly into slumber.

The siren of a police car pulling up to the curb awakens him to reality, and a voice calls to those faceless beings who slow down to watch, "NOTHING TO SEE HERE FOLKS, JUST MOVE ALONG!"

Helping him into the back seat of the cruiser, they pull away from the curb, leaving behind a pile of rags and newspapers. His bed.

Nothing to see here folks, just move along.

The Throw-Away People

IMA Live

SHE CLIMBED THE CREAKY old stairs of the even older, creepy mansion filled with odd people of various sorts, on her way to her therapist's room on the third floor. She knocked. He answered, bidding her to enter. As she sat in the lumpy fake-leather, now-familiar, brown chair, she began her session. About 3 hours later, it was time to leave, to join the other poor, huddled women and men, young and old – her friends and fellow passengers on the voyage to the promised land of normal mental health. Before leaving the room, she looked again at the faded poster on the far wall. A drawing of a dog stared back at her. The caption under the dog informed her that he had three legs, was missing an ear, was blind in one eye, and had just been castrated. The dog's name was "Lucky." She smiled again at the irony.

She began to reach for the doorknob and then, turning back, asked him the question that had been niggling at the back of her mind for these past 27 days. She asked him why it was that she could spend 2-3 hours a day with him – where he found this luxurious and vital time just for her when her time was set for 50 minutes. He said that that he took the time from the other people, the people that he said were "not going to make it," so that he could rescue those who could. She thought that he had certainly rescued her, at least temporarily, from the whirlpool of despair that they call depression before it had sucked her down totally and finally. She was indeed one lucky dog. She thanked him and left.

As she descended the stairs, creaking with every second or third step, she considered. She was almost ready to leave the old mansion again, pick up the pieces of her real life. She knew that she was going to make it this time, for six or seven months at least. But what about Sally, her basketball buddy, who had beaten her countless times in the make-shift court in the old yard?

What about Fred, who professed his love to her but was always tearfully pleading for her not to kill him, that he was not a Nazi, and to hook him up to the lie-detector (actually a VCR player on the little TV) and that she could see that he was telling her the truth. She would tell him again that afternoon that she believed him and would never hurt him. Again, he would look at her doubtfully.

What about June, her sweet, pleasant room-mate, who sometimes listened to the voices that only she could hear that told her to press the cigarette to the battle-scarred flesh of her arm? What about the somewhat smelly old man without his dentures, who stole her book whenever he could? What about the three women that worked with her in the flower garden? What about all the others, fighting depression, mania, or other forms of insanity? Most of them were Throw-Away People who had lost their time in therapy to her or the other, privileged few who were deemed able to recover enough to live in some meaningful way at least part of the time. They would die, but she would live, partially because of their unwitting (literally) sacrifice of their time with Tom, who decided who would have his time and attention and who would be sucked down forever into the icy waters of despair.

As she left the mansion yet again on this coming Wednesday, she knew that again she would look back and figuratively downward. She was like Charleton Heston in *Ben Hurr*, glancing back at those still straining at their oars, chained to the ship until the battle was finally lost and they descended into the ocean's unforgiving depths.

She thought that she should feel guilty for taking their time with Tom, but she could only be grateful that she was not thrown away too.

OTHER WORLDS

Stories that take place in worlds other than our own!

Adelaide, The Bookbinder by Alexxa Burton

The Orphaned Twins by Crystal Hoff

A "Real" Golf Story by Bill Reid

Adelaide, The Bookbinder

Alexxa Burton

HER JOURNAL WAS GONE. The one that had been sitting on her desk. The one that she wrote her private thoughts, observations about the world and, most embarrassingly, her poetry in. The one that was the same color of green as her ink well. And her favorite dress. The dress she was wearing, the dress that looked so lovely against her dark skin. The one that was the exact same leather she'd used making the handcrafted books she had shipped out to the bookseller last night.

Adelaide froze. She'd known when that beautiful green leather had come into the shop that she shouldn't use it for herself. But it was such beautiful leather, so soft, and the exact shade of dark green that was her favorite. Carefully, she had cut just enough to make one single notebook. By the light of an oil lamp, she'd folded the pages and stitched the binding. Adelaide was a bookbinder by trade, the best in the city. Books she'd made were on the shelves of every high-end bookseller around. The notebook she had made was simple, plain: no fancy leatherwork stamped into the cover, no gold leaf on the binding. But it was beautiful in its simplicity. And it was almost exactly like the books that had been shipped out yesterday.

Was it possible the stockboy Michael had seen it on her desk and thought it was supposed to be part of the shipment? He must have. It was the only thing that made sense.

Adelaide grabbed her black cloak and her bag, packed with her inkwell for her plans to go down to the river this morning and write, and took off out the door, hardly remembering to lock it behind her.

She rushed through the streets in the dawn light. The bookseller was clear on the other end of the city. She would have hired a cab, but few were running this early.

Adelaide stopped at a corner and looked to the left. Perhaps she should head to Michael's first. He lived just down this street. Perhaps he hadn't put her journal into the shipment of books, perhaps there was another explanation. Hopeful, she turned to the left.

Even rushing as she was, the sun had finished rising by the time she was knocking on Michael's door. Her first, polite knock received no response and in her desperation she found herself knocking harder, and then banging on Michael's door. When Michael finally came to the door it was clear she had woken him. He was holding a housecoat closed around him and rubbing his eyes, still blurry from sleep.

"Miss Adelaide? Was I supposed to be at work this morning?"

"No Michael, there's no work today."

"I thought I was in trouble there for a moment Miss."

"Michael, did you take a book off my desk yesterday?"

"A green one, Miss. One of the ones we were shipping to the High Dtreet bookseller. I almost missed it sitting there. It was the last one I put in the box. Wouldn't want the shipment to be a book short."

Adelaide closed her eyes. "No, we wouldn't want that indeed, Michael. Thank you for letting me know. Enjoy your day off. I'm sorry for waking you so early."

"Have a good day, Miss Adelaide," said Michael, and he closed the door.

Adelaide stood there on the stoop for a moment, any hope that her journal was somehow still in her possession dashed. She began walking back to the main road, hoping to make it to the bookseller's before he realized her journal had been included in his shipment. Or worse- before he sold it.

It was a long walk across the city, and the streets were bustling by the time she got there.

Adelaide had her hand on the handle of the bookshop door when she let out a cry of anguish. The shop was closed, the windows dark and the door locked. A piece of paper tacked to the door read, *Out of town for a family emergency. Back in a week. Sorry for the inconvenience.*

She rattled the door in frustration but it was useless. Then a thought jumped into her head, *Doesn't he just live around the corner? Maybe he hasn't left yet.*

She knew he had still been in the city the night before to take possession of the book shipment.

Adelaide hurried down the street and rounded the corner to knock on another door.

As she knocked, she could hear noises from within the house. Her heart was in her throat. *Please let him not have left yet.*

A woman opened the door, holding a baby, with two toddlers clinging to her skirts. "Miss Adelaide?" said the woman in confusion, exhaustion apparent in her voice though it was just barely noon.

"Mrs... " Adelaide struggled to remember the bookseller's last name.

"Just call me Mary, dear. Thomas isn't here. He left out first thing this morning. Something about securing a new book before he leaves town. We just got word yesterday his sister has fallen ill."

"The shipment I sent over yesterday, do you know where it might be?"

"I'm not sure dear. It's as much as I can do to keep my head on straight with these three. I think he may have sent some of it out this morning. I know he was in the shop till after midnight last night. If you'd like, I can send word when he gets back into town?"

"Yes please, thank you, Mary. I appreciate that very much. I'm sorry to bother you, Mary."

"It's no bother at all Miss Adelaide. Sorry I couldn't help more." Mary closed the door. Adelaide stood there, staring at the ground in disappointment.

Slowly, Adelaide turned and started on the long trip home.

It took her longer to get home than the trip to the bookbinder's. Adelaide walked slowly, looking at the ground, not at all taking in the beauty of the day. She passed by people, never noticing their faces, never noticing the hundreds of tiny things that would normally bring her joy.

She passed by the river, passed by the very spot she had planned to sit with her journal that morning. The spot that provided a perfect view of the river, with the peaceful, kinetic frenzy of its running water, and a perfect view of the street and its people, with a kinetic, frenzied energy all their own. She passed that spot without even looking up.

Even the scents of food from the various shops she passed did nothing to pull her out of her doldrums.

Walking across the city and back had taken most of the day, a day that had seemed so full of promise when she'd gotten out of bed. How quickly things change.

Adelaide knew that losing her journal really was a small thing, but knowing it was out of her possession, that her innermost thoughts were out there in the world, unguarded... She felt exposed and vulnerable.

It was evening before she turned onto her own street, her feet dragging as she plodded homeward. Adelaide didn't look up until she was at the steps of the building that was both her home and her shop.

Sitting there on the steps, flipping through the pages of a book, was the bookseller. Flipping through the pages of her book.

Mortification struck her like a ton of bricks. This man was reading her journal. Reading *her* journal!

"Ah, Miss Adelaide! I've been waiting for you. You see, I happened to come into possession of the most marvelous book, just a first draft mind you, but so full of potential I had to secure it before any of my competitors stumbled upon it. *The Musings and Poetry of Miss Adelaide*. It has a certain ring to it, don't you think?

"Now, this draft has some more private bits that I skipped over for courtesy, but the public observations, poetry, and prose are quite captivating."

Adelaide's jaw fell. He wanted to sell her poems. He thought her thoughts were "captivating"? And her private thoughts were still safe. If he had read them, he was at least being polite about it. "You want to sell my book?" she stammered.

"Yes, very much so, Miss Adelaide. In fact, I'd like an exclusive contract. And I can see a second and third volume in the future. After you finish this one of course. There seem to be quite a few empty pages yet to fill."

"Yes, yes, of course. I'll get right to work." The words cascaded from her mouth like the water in the river.

"And I trust you to design the binding," he smiled. "I believe you're in the acquaintance of a very talented young bookbinder."

"I'll have it to you as soon as I can, Sir."

"No rush. I must leave town tonight but I'll drop by to see how it's going when I get back. If that's alright of course?"

"My thoughts are with your sister. I spoke with your wife today."

"Thank you, Miss Adelaide." Thomas stood and handed her the green leather notebook. "I will be seeing you in the near future then." He walked past her and down the street, leaving her with her thoughts.

Adelaide stood there at the steps of her home, her journal safe in her own hands, still in shock.

How quickly things change indeed.

The Orphaned Twins

Crystal Hoff

THE SNOWFALL KINGDOM AND Taryn Kingdom had been at war for many decades because of a family feud that couldn't be buried. The warring kingdom belonged to the Snowfall Kingdom's King's brother.

When the deaf King and blind Queen of Snowfall Kingdom were blessed to have twin boys they named Donald and Duke, they were born deaf. But, that didn't matter to their parents who loved them all the same.

When the twins turned five their lives would be turned upside down.

Their parents went out to fight in the war, to protect their kingdom and their sons, but they never returned. This left the boys orphaned. The boys were too young to understand what was really happening.

The King's brother came in and took over the throne, shipping his nephews to a poor orphanage in a neighboring country.

Life in the orphanage wasn't easy on the twins. Most nights they went to bed hungry or they were bullied because nobody understood sign language.

One night, while everyone was asleep, the twins snuck out of the orphanage and onto the cold, snowy streets.

Duke signed to Donald, *I'm scared what's going to happen to us now?*

Donald signed back and said, *I know Duke. I'm scared too. I don't know what's going to happen, but as long as we're together, we'll be alright.*

That night they slept in an old cardboard box in an alley.

The next morning a caring, elderly shop owner, Nicolas, found the two boys sleeping next door to his store. It broke his heart just thinking these kids had no place to spend Christmas.

So when the boys awoke the elderly man asked his wife to invite them to come into their shop and join them for breakfast.

The boys agreed as they hadn't eaten anything since the night before. When the elderly man put down the food in front of the boys they scarfed it down.

He asked them how long it'd been since they'd eaten a good, home cooked meal.

But, when he didn't get an answer his wife used sign language to communicate with the boys. *How long has it been since you've had a good, home cooked meal?*

Donald signed back to the shop keepers wife, *We haven't had a good meal since we've been at the orphanage.*

How would you two like to spend the Christmas Holidays with us? she asked.

We would love too are you sure we don't want to be a burden to you.

She responded, *We miss hearing little feet running across the floor. It's been lonely for us. How about we get you two in a bath and get you some clean clothes?*

Duke nodded, ready to get out of his old raggedy ones.

So, the shop keepers wife helped the boys with their bath and got them changed. She sat down with them and taught them how to talk and use their voices. It didn't take long for Donald to start talking to the shop keeper and his wife, but Duke had always been the quiet shy one out of the twins. The shop keeper's wife understood where Duke was coming from - she was once quiet and shy herself.

Later that night, the boys cuddled up with Nicolas and his wife in front of a roaring fire place.

Christmas was getting closer, and the couple decided to adopt the boys and welcome them into their family.

When the boys found out they were being adopted by the couple they both started crying happy tears. They hugged the their new parents and were finally able to have a home again where they'd be loved and cherished.

They would never be alone ever again.

A "Real" Golf Story

Bill Reid

I suppose that most people reading this story are familiar with at least a few golf terms, such as 'birdy,' 'eagle,' 'par,' 'tee-box.' This story is the origin of the term 'par.'

A long time ago in a galaxy far, far away... sorry, wrong story. Anyways, there lived in the northern part of England, near the Scottish border, a notorious highway man known as 'Philip of Parr.'

Now, Philip was not a run of the mill highwayman[1], especially not of this era. No long, scraggly hair, no gaunt body, no bad complexion or horrible teeth. On the contrary, he had long, wavy, blonde hair, blue eyes, and chiseled features that came from his Norse ancestors. He was the perfect picture of an aristocrat, with charm to spare, that a few of the young lassies that lived in the surrounding countryside would testify to (but that would be a story for a more racy crowd).

Philip's charm and aristocratic looks were the reason he could gain the confidence of the travelling merchants that plied their trade along the roads between England and Scotland.

While Philip socialized among the merchants and travelers with drink and food, Philip's gang of highwaymen would be hiding in the surrounding woods. And at just the right moment- the gang would attack! After relieving the confused victims of their gold and silver, Philip and his gang would retreat posthaste back to their hideout among the hills of northern England.

To keep the traveling merchants off balance, Philip would periodically change tactics. Along with his extraordinary charm, Philip was a master of disguise. He would

---

1. A highwayman is a person who threatens and steals from people going along the road.

portray a merchant, a weary traveler, a poor pilgrim, an officer of the crown, even a "man of the cloth."

The tactics would change, but the results would be the same: Philip's gang heading back to their hideout, loaded down with their plunder, nothing left behind but a group of humiliated victims holding empty money bags.

The only exception was Philip himself. To keep his identity a secret, he would slip away during the apex of the melee between his gang and the merchants, then rejoin his highwaymen along the trail back to the hills.

Philip's actions were reaching proportions so serious that it drew the attention of the Crown. The King was receiving scathing reports from the angry merchants and the small hamlets scattered around the countryside (but to the King, his biggest concern was losing the tax money from the merchants).

In response to these complaints, the King dispatched a highly-trained regiment of troops to round up Philip and his gang. As the troops scoured the countryside, Philip's band escaped into the hills and glens of southern Scotland. The English troops secured the border, which meant that Philip could not resume his thieving ways. It wasn't long before there was grumbling among the gang- Philip was running short of coin!

Philip searched for another way to resume his career. At this time golf was becoming a national past time of Scotland. It was played by the very wealthy, and Philip had a plan to fill his empty coffers. The gang would lie in wait while Philip charmed his way into the players' confidence. When the moment was right, they would swoop down on their victims, relieve them of their coin, then disappear back into the hills.

This would be repeated all throughout central and southern Scotland. Eventually, the local authorities decided on a plan to stop this thieving band. They hired local ruffians [2] of their own, dressed them as 'dandies[3],' then sent them out to trap the "Parr Gang."

Weeks passed as the ruffians travelled around the golf links, trying to lure Philip and his cohorts out into the open. Then, one late afternoon, on a remote green of a large course, the Parr Gang attacked the so-called dandies. A furious battle broke out as another group of ruffians joined the frey. The Parr Gang was driven back into the hills, but not before leaving four Parr members dispatched into the darkness of evil.

---

2. The local ruffians were paid, but were further controlled with the threat of being '"pressed" into service with the English Navy and/or a merchant fleet

3. "Dandy" was a slang term for a well dressed, wealthy person

Now, this green would come to be known as the "4 Parr Hole." From then on, the players would try to play the hole in four shots, and as they say, the rest is history. So was the Parr Gang, as they ceased to exist.

A couple months after the defeat of Parr Gang, a young lad came running into the clubhouse, exclaiming, "I shot a birdie on the 4 Parr Hole!"

"How did you do that?" clamored the crowd.

The lad explained that while his hitting his third shot, a large bird swooped down and landed beside the hole. As the ball came down, it hit the unfortunate fowl in the head. The ball bounced off his head and into the hole for a 3. Again, as they say, the rest is history. So was the bird.

This story was told to me by a very famous "storyteller," a descendent of a very long line of storytellers. As for Philip, he vanished like a puff of smoke, never to be seen again in the British Isles...

Although, from time to time, there would be reports of a suave gentleman with long, wavy, blonde hair and blue eyes, travelling the waters and the islands of the Caribbean.

The end?

Ask the storytellers.

KINDLING

Tales that include the powerful element of fire.

Fire Flight by Alexxa Burton

AfterFlare: Mike Harden's Journal

Fire Flight

Alexxa Burton

Author's note: This story takes place on the planet Miaca. For more adventures exploring Miaca, check out the novel, *From Winter,* and short story, *Half-Blood.*

"Why did we have to leave the festival so early papa?"

"It's already far past your bedtime, Alaia. Little girls should be in bed."

"Can we go back tomorrow, papa? I want to see a sietara corone." He smiled. Sietaras were the largest of the three species of burning birds, large enough to carry a person on their backs as they flew. He knew they fascinated her and she wanted to fly through the sky on the back of her very own sietara. The festival they had just left was the SchewdaeCoshcona marking the start of the burning birds' breeding season in late spring after the windstorms had ended for the year and Miaca's skies were peaceful again.

"If you're good, we can go back tomorrow. Maybe if you're extra good, you can even hold a cheo." Cheos were the smallest of the burning birds, about the size of an adult's hand. There was always a privately owned flock or two roaming the festival grounds during the Schewdae-Coshcona for festivalgoers' enjoyment.

"'If I'm extra, extra, extra good, can I RIDE a sietara tomorrow?"

"I think maybe you have to be at least as old as Kai'ano was when she first rode one. Do you know who Kai'ano was?"

Alaia shook her head.

"Well hurry up and get ready for bed, then I'll tell you all about her."

"I'll be so fast papa!" And with that Alaia ran off to change for bed.

Mazon, Alaia's father, laughed to himself and walked down the hall after her.

"I'm ready papa!" called Alaia.

"Are you now?" Mazon asked, sitting on the edge of her bed. He helped Alaia straighten her top, which was on backwards, and take the braids out of her hair, then lifted her into bed. "All ready for your story now?"

"Yes papa." She looked at him with bright, eager eyes.

"A long time ago, before Miaca sent ships to the stars, before even the people of Miaca had come together as one planet, over a thousand years ago, when the only way to get around was riding on the back of a prehliq, there was a little girl named Kai'ano. She was 12 years old and lived with her family outside of the town that would someday become the Tor'B'acoe, but back then it was just a town and not the capital city of the southern continent.

"Kai'ano's family were fruit famers and had a large orchard filled with fruit trees and terian berry bramble vines. Kai'ano loved to go out into the back of the orchard where the trees were the tallest, and the terian vines were the thickest, and eat berries until her hands and face were stained yellow from their juice.

"That's a little bit like another girl we know, isn't it?"

"I love terian berries papa!"

"I know you do!

"Almost every afternoon Kai'ano would sneak off to the back of the orchard where her parents rarely went. The only days she didn't go were days it was raining, or snowing, or if she thought there might be a spring windstorm.

"On the southern continent the windstorms are much worse than they are up here in the north. There's large swaths of open desert in the south with nothing to stop the winds from blowing straight through.

"Kai'ano was afraid of the windstorms, so she always stayed inside, hidden safe in her bed when they came."

"I don't like the windstorms either papa. They could pick me up and blow me away!"

"I'd never let that happen, kaba."

"Don't call me "kaba", I'm not little anymore!"

"You're right Alaia, you're almost 7 now, you're a big girl."

Alaia nodded indignantly. "And soon I'll be 12 like Kai'ano and I can ride a sietara corone too!"

"Once you're 12 like Kai'ano.

"One day, early in the spring, there wasn't much fruit on the trees and they'd only just had the first windstorm of the season. Kai'ano put on her shoes and jacket and started walking to the back orchard. She was hoping to find a few of her favorite terian berries ready to eat on the vines.

"The terian vines grew wild between the fruit trees, right up to, and up, their trunks. The thorn covered vines made it hard to walk through the trees and collect their fruit at harvest, but they protected the trees' fruit from animals that would otherwise eat a large portion of the valuable harvest. They did little though to stop a determined girl. Kai'ano usually spent the whole summer with her arms and legs scratched up from climbing around in those vines in search of berries.

"She made the long walk out to the back orchard. Out of the yard, past the pond, jumping over the little stream where she knew just which rocks on its banks were slippery and should be avoided being stepped on. She could make this walk with her eyes closed.

"Kai'ano reached the back orchard to find most of the berries still small and underripe, but buried deep within the thorns near the base of one single tree were several bunches of perfectly ripe golden berries.

"She crawled her way back to them, the thorns of the vines catching on her clothes and hair, scratching her skin, but she didn't notice. She sat with her back against the trunk of the tree, picking the terian berries one by one and eating them, savoring the tart flavor of the early berries.

"Between the shelter of her little cave of thorns and the distraction of the berries, she didn't notice the sky changing. It was slowly going from the soft, blue lavender of a gentle spring day to a steely gray color. If Kai'ano had happened to look up she would have known instantly that this color meant a windstorm was on its way and she would have made her way safely home as quickly as she could. But she didn't look up, feeling happy and safe in her hideaway, thinking herself still wrapped in the calm spring day she had stepped out into that afternoon.

"Even the first few gusts of wind did nothing to raise her awareness of the brewing situation.

"It wasn't until her hair was getting whipped around her face and tangled in the thorns that she noticed the danger rapidly growing around her.

"Kai'ano knew there wasn't time to get back home before the storm arrived in full force. She doubted she could even make it to the barn or equipment shed which were much closer. And being caught out in the open during a windstorm wasn't something she wanted to risk. She looked around her trying to gauge how much shelter the cave of vines and fruit trees offered her, if she should stay where she was, or try to make a run for the shed. A sudden gust of wind pushing her back against the tree let her know the time to make that decision was past. Her only option was to stay where she was and hope for the best.

"She saw the tree had an exposed root so she tied herself to it with her jacket. It was a large tree and its roots ran deep.

"Kai'ano closed her eyes, shaking in terror and hugging the tree as the winds picked up. Her hair blew wildly around her and bits of debris stung her skin. Some of the terian berry vines were ripped from the ground. They whipped around, their thorns like sharp little weapons biting into her exposed skin. Kai'ano clung to the tree too afraid to open her eyes. Any noise or cry she made was carried away by the wind before it reached her ears.

"Suddenly she heard crashing through the trees and feral screaming. Kai'ano dared to open her eyes just a sliver, for a single moment, and saw a flash of something orange being blown, crashing past her through the orchard. She couldn't make out what it was but it was big, and as scared as she was. There was nothing she could do but hold on to the tree and wait for the winds to stop.

"She had no idea how long she was trapped there, clinging to the tree in terror. It felt like hours but windstorms, while violent, rarely lasted that long, usually no more than an hour before blowing themselves out or rushing past to a new place.

"Kai'ano stayed there, still clinging to the tree for her life, for long moments after the wind had died down, unable and unwilling to release her grasp. Slowly her breathing and heartbeat returned to normal and she was able to open her eyes again.

"The world around her was largely unchanged by the storm. The vines around her were a bit messier, the path she had forged into them to get all the way back to the berries had been destroyed, but the orchard still stood. The tree she clung to still stood.

"Kai'ano untied herself and fought her way out through the tangle of vines. Her arms and face were covered in small cuts from the thorns, and bleeding, but not too badly. Some soap, water, and ointment would have her put right in no time.

"She could hear an odd noise farther back in the orchard, a sort of low screeching. It sounded exhausted and in pain. Kai'ano remembered the orange thing that had crashed past her in the storm and went carefully to investigate. She had walked no more than five or six rows of trees farther back when she saw, tangled in vines and trapped between two trees that were particularly close together, suspended upsidedown by the vines entangling it, a young but fully grown sietara corone.

"Kai'ano froze. She had never seen a sietara before. They rarely came this far down out of the wooded mountains. It was huge, even bigger than the prehliqs in the barn that she and her family rode to and from town.

"His feathers were covered in dirt and debris from the storm but there was no mistaking the shifting orange, yellow, and red colors of the feathers that gave the birds their name. She didn't know what to do. The bird was clearly trapped and injured, its left wing sticking out an odd angle. She stood watching it, and it watching her.

"You've heard sietara corone are very smart. Domestic ones have been found to be able to form a sort of bond, communication, with their handlers on almost a telepathic level.

"As Kai'ano and this bird looked at each other, her arm slowly began to ache, her left arm, like the bird's left wing, and she slowly became aware of a feeling of great need deep within her, the need for help, the sietara's need for help.

"Hesitantly, one step at a time, Kai'ano moved closer to the unmoving sietara as it continued to watch her. Kai'ano knew that animals which were afraid or in pain were prone to snapping, so she stayed clear of its large, sharp beak, the size of her arm, even though so far the great bird had remained still and calm, although never taking his eyes off her. Bit by bit she disentangled the sietara from the vines. She hesitated again before freeing his head but he never once made a move to snap or bite her and soon the bird was sitting comfortably on the ground.

"Kai'ano expected him to fly away once she'd freed him but he continued to sit there just staring at her. As she looked into the bird's eyes, she felt a sudden stab of pain in her arm again.

"Was the bird telling her his wing was broken? Kai'ano eyed the sietara's wing skeptically. She once had set the wing of one of the coresiets her family owned when a predator had gotten into the coop, but she didn't know if she could do the same for something this large.

"She reached out a hand toward the sietara but didn't step forward. Now that he was free, she didn't know if he would still let her touch him.

"He turned his head to the side away from the affected wing as if to put his threatening beak as far away as possible. She moved forward and slowly, carefully, felt her way down the bones that made up the huge wing. She felt a shift in the bone in the lower part of the wing, what would have been her forearm, and felt the bird's whole body tense as she probed it. It was indeed broken.

"Kai'ano was still unsure if she could set it but felt she had to try. Taking stock of the huge bird's beak which was still stretched as far away from her as could be, and his talons, each the size of her hand, which were firmly tucked under his body, she slowly stretched the wing out straight to allow her to align the bone properly.

"The bird pressed his head low to the ground as if he knew what was coming. She looked at him one more time before making the swift sudden movement that would set the bone. The sietara screamed. That same horrible painful scream she'd heard when he'd tumbled past her in the storm, but he made no move to bite or otherwise injure her.

"Kai'ano carefully guided the bird's wing back against his body. She didn't know how to secure it. With the coresiet they'd bandaged the wing to the bird's body to hold it in place while it healed but she had no bandages with her and the sietara was so much bigger. She tried to tie her jacket around the bird's body but it wasn't very effective.

"She stood back just looking at the bird again. He had just told her his wing was broken, and somehow, he had realized she feared his beak and talons, so perhaps she could tell him not to move it. She looked deep into his eyes and tried to send the sense to him of holding her own arm very still, not moving it no matter what. After several minutes she felt a sense of understanding wash over her.

Was it her imagination or was the sietara really telling her he understood what she was trying to tell him?

"Kai'ano looked around. It was getting dark. Her parents would be worried if she wasn't home soon. Probably already were worried, when she hadn't returned after the storm.

"'I'll be back first thing in the morning' she said aloud to the bird, then turned and ran for the cottage trying to beat the sunset.

"Her parents had been very worried about her, because that's what parents do when something bad could have happened to their children, and when she got home they gave her lots of hugs and told her how scared they'd been." Mazon looked down at Alaia who sleepily nodded back at him, fighting to stay awake for the rest of the story.

"That night Kai'ano looked out her window into the darkness thinking of the sietara corone. Would he still be there when she got there in the morning? Could he leave with that broken wing? If he was there, he would need food. He couldn't hunt if he couldn't fly. She'd have to bring him food. She'd need to bring him water too. How much did a bird that size need to eat?

"She fell asleep busy making plans for the morning.

"Kai'ano woke up with the sun, but had to wait until after breakfast with her parents to head out to the back orchard. She could hardly sit still in her chair with anticipation. Kai'ano hadn't told her parents about the sietara.

She didn't know why. She knew she wouldn't be in trouble but she was afraid they might not let her go back or that other people might come and take the sietara away.

"Slipping out the door as soon as she was able, her first stop was the family coresiet coop. Kai'ano caught one of the round, lumpy, flightless birds, and tucked it under her arm. She had picked an older bird that had stopped laying eggs long ago. The next stop was the equipment shed where she took a bucket and two of the traps that they used to keep predators out of the coresiet coop. Her arms full, she made her way to the back orchard, pausing again only to fill her bucket with water from the stream.

"She could see his bright orange feathers from a distance as she approached. He was still there! Kai'ano wanted to run but she didn't, for fear of spilling her bucket or losing the wriggling coresiet still tucked under her arm.

"'Hi, how's your wing?' she asked as she approached. 'I brought you something to eat.' She set the traps and bucket down and considered how to best offer the sietara the coresiet and decided to try simply setting it down within reach of the larger bird, then stepping back to give the sietara some room. He snapped, picking up his meal and swallowing it whole.

"Kai'ano then offered the bucket of water. The sietara contemplated the water and how to fit his beak into the bucket.

"'Um... how about this?' She picked the bucket up again and closed her eyes, picturing pouring the water into the sietara's beak. When she opened her eyes, he was holding his head low to the ground with his beak open and slowly, one beakfull at a time, he drank the whole bucket of water.

"When they were done, he slowly reached his beak out to Kai'ano and waited for her to place her hand on it. They stayed like that for a moment, the large bird expressing his thanks.

"'You need a name. I can't keep thinking of you as "the sietara."' She sat on the ground and they contemplated each other. 'Um... I like the name Zilan, how about you?"'

"The bird let out a quiet screech.

"'I'll take that as a yes.' She stood up again. 'I have to go. I have to set the traps to catch you more food. I can't keep giving you coresiets or my family won't have any eggs. I'll try and come back tonight but if I can't, I'll definitely be back tomorrow.' She grabbed the bucket and traps, and ran back toward the cottage, almost forgetting to stop to set the traps elsewhere in the orchard.

"She knew a broken bone would take several weeks to heal and hoped she could catch enough to feed Zilan that long.

"Spring got warmer and the trees in the orchard were covered with flowers, insects were everywhere pollinating the flowers. There would be an abundance of fruit in the summer and fall.

"Every day, Kai'ano went to the back orchard, checking the traps and filling her bucket with water along the way. She had eight traps set through the orchard by now and was usually able to bring Zilan two or three small animals a day.

"Thankfully, the windstorms were mostly mild for the rest of the season as Kai'ano had no idea how she would have protected Zilan against another bad one in his mostly immobile condition. He could walk of course, and after the first day or two he did, following Kai'ano to the stream and drinking on his own, but every day when she went out, she still found him waiting without fail in that spot she'd first found him.

"She spent hours in the back orchard with Zilan and crawling around in the briars picking terian berries. She talked to him for hours and at times, more often than not, he seemed to understand, interacting, and responding, trying to communicate back as best he could. Sometimes Kai'ano would find pictures or emotions in her head that weren't hers and though she had no proof she assumed they came from Zilan. Kai'ano was quickly coming to consider the big bird her best friend. She tried to not think about the coming day when his wing would be healed and he would be strong enough to fly back to the woods and mountains.

"Every day he grew a bit stronger, following her around the orchard on her search for berries, even catching some small prey animals on his own. Zilan began following her to the stream every time she left to go back to the cottage, and every time they reached the stream she would stop, look into his eyes, telling him to go back, to not follow her any further, and picturing the orchard.

"She feared if her parents knew she had befriended the large bird, they would be afraid and not let her go out to the orchard alone any longer. As close as she and Zilan had become, sietara corone were still predators, large enough he could have done her serious damage in a single moment. Kai'ano knew Zilan would never hurt her but at times that long sharp beak the size of her arm, and razor sharp talons the size of her hand, still gave her pause.

"Spring was ending, with summer coming soon. She knew Zilan's wing was healing and he would be flying again soon. More than once she had seen images from high in the sky, felt the wind on her face and the sensation of her arms pumping to keep her aloft. There was happiness in those images, but sadness too. He didn't want to leave her behind any more than she wanted him to go.

"But the day finally came when Kai'ano reached the back orchard and Zilan wasn't there. Kai'ano's face fell. She sat on the ground with her back to one of the trees Zilan had been pinned to when she'd first found him. She didn't want to believe he was gone.

"Kai'ano was looking at the ground thinking of her friend. She wasn't watching the sky. Why would she watch the sky? She was used to seeing Zilan on the ground so she was surprised by a sudden loud rustling behind her.

"She looked up and shrieked. Zilan had just landed behind her. She jumped up and ran to him, throwing her arms around his neck. 'You can fly again!'

"He made soft bird noises in his throat as if he was speaking back.

"'I know you have to fly away and go home but I was so sad thinking I didn't even get to say goodbye.'

"Zilan lowered his head over her shoulder as if hugging her back. Then he gently nudged her, pushing her back, along his neck.

"Kai'ano looked up at him, confused. 'What do you want Zi?'

"He continued to push her back toward his shoulder.

"'I don't understand.'

"She then felt the wind on her face and saw the ground as if high above like he had shown her so many times before. But Kai'ano kept looking at Zilan, not understanding what he was trying to tell her. To move so he could fly away maybe? She tried to step back away from him but he wouldn't let her. Then she felt a weight on her shoulders and understood.

"'You want me to ride you?' She had never heard of such a thing, never thought of such a thing. No one had ever ridden a sietara before. As far as she knew, no one had befriended one, or had even been close to one, either. She looked around, unsure. 'So how do I do this?' she asked mostly herself.

"Zilan laid his body as flat on the ground as he could and Kai'ano struggled to pull herself up without tugging too hard on his feathers. She didn't want to hurt him.

"When at last she was seated securely, her knees tucked just behind his wing joints, Zilan looked back at her, meeting her eyes with eyes that held a depth of intelligence and emotion that she'd never consciously noticed before. He looked at her as if to say 'Hold on.' She could almost hear him speak it.

"Then he looked forward and Kai'ano could feel his muscles tense and ripple under her. He raised up, getting to his feet, then launched himself into the air. There was no gradual graceful lift off, just a thrust and fury of wings, and they were aloft, high in the sky above the trees.

"Kai'ano buried her face in Zilan's neck feathers, afraid to look, but hiding her eyes did no good as he put the images of what he was seeing straight into her mind. Slowly she lifted her head to peer over his shoulder. They were so high up! She could see everything! Her cottage, the mountains, the forest, the town, and they'd flown so far already. They were already over the town after only a few minutes. It usually took half a day to walk there. Kai'ano sat up straight to get a better look around. It was amazing! The view, soaring through the sky, feeling Zilan beneath her, the wind in her hair, all of it! She wanted to stay in the sky forever.

"Zilan seemed aware of her racing thoughts, and images started coming to her of mountains, cliffs, forests, open meadows, of his home in the mountains. The images shifted as if it were her and him melded together, flying in the mountains, seeing small shapes on the distant ground, itching to grab them, suddenly diving down, falling down at the ground, grasping with hands, or rather talons, at just the right moment to catch some wriggling thing, and leveling out to race along the ground with their prize firmly in their grasp. In the vision, they angled into the open sky again as a forest of trees rushed toward them letting their speed die off enough to turn, then seeing a nest on a far-off cliff. Zilan's home, she knew.

"Her exhilaration seemed to feed his, and his hers. The images changed and they were racing along the side of a mountain when suddenly the ground disappeared from beneath them, they'd screamed off the edge of a cliff! They dove steeply again, down and down endlessly, rocketing faster and faster, vision blurring, toward a bottom she almost couldn't see anymore, then in an instant shot out, parallel to the ground, moving at immense speed across the treetops, everything blurred except for another cliff ahead, and in another instant they were climbing up and up along the cliff-face, finally slowing, coming almost to a pause, starting to sink back to the ground, but her talons latching onto something, the nest! Then, almost carefully turning and looking out over miles and miles of meadows and rocks and forests, a map of the world, her world, rolled out before her. Zilan's home in the mountains.

"And then...

"Then her sight was her own again and Zilan was climbing over the town far, far below, receding to look so small. Then suddenly, just as at the cliff, he dove down at the town. For one horrifying moment she thought he meant to scoop up a townsperson for dinner but he leveled off over the rooftops. They were so close she could nearly reach out and touch them, she could read the signs on the shops, and see the people in the streets. Then they were climbing again.

"Zilan flew her around until the sun went down, landing again in the back orchard.

"Kai'ano was sad as they landed. She knew now that Zilan would leave and go home to the nest on that cliff, and she was likely to never see him again.

"She slid off his back and hugged him around the neck, then let go and looked up at him. 'I'll never forget you.'

"Zilan turned as if preening himself, and pulled out two of his wing feathers laying them at Kai'ano's feet. They were almost as long as she was tall. Sietara feathers were very valuable. Kai'ano knew that just one of these could bring her family more money than the fruit harvest for the next two years. Is that why he'd given her two? One to sell and one to keep? To remember him by? She hugged him again, then watched as he flew away toward the mountains.

"The people in town had seen Kai'ano's flight through the sky on Zilan's back. They said they looked like a streak of fire in the sky and after that, every year on that day, we have celebrated the burning birds and that first flight Kai'ano and Zilan took together with the SchewdaeCoshcona.

"And Kai'ano did see Zilan again. Every year he came back to the orchard and the two of them would go flying together again over the town."

Mazon looked down at Alaia who had long since fallen asleep. He had known she had, he had finished the story anyway. Someday she would stay awake for the whole thing. He smiled and tucked her into bed. Looking back one more time before he shut the door, he smiled, anticipating her face when she saw the sietara corones flying over the city tomorrow.

Glossary

cheoe: spark, as in "spark bird"
pronounced "**KEY-oh**"

corone: bird
pronounced "**cor-RONE**"

coresiet: Literally "home bird" a flightless, egg producing bird often kept by Miacon households.
pronounced "**CORE-sight**"

kaba: term of endearment for children, roughly translates to "little one".
pronounced "**KAY-bah**"

prehliq: an animal used for pulling carts or riding much like a horse in size but more goat-like in appearance.
pronounced "**PRAY-(Lee-q)**"

SchewdaeCoshcona: Literally, "Festival of Fire." Celebrates the burning birds. Takes place in late spring.
pronounced "**Shoe-dae-coash-CON-a**".

sietara: Blaze, as in "blaze bird" the largest of the three species of burning birds.
pronounced "**zee-TAR-uh**"

terian: a type of golden berries that grow on thorny vines and ripen through the spring and summer.

pronounced "**TEAR-re-in**"

Tor'B'acoe: Literally "second heart", the capital city of the southern continent.

pronounced "**dTor-Bee-AYKO**"

AfterFlare: Mike Harden's Journal

Lisa A. Beltz

MAY 25, 31 AF

After much soul-searching, I begin this journal attempting to put into words humanity's path in this brave/cowardly new world, hoping to gain insights into what led to the collapse of the former world and the birth of the new and make peace with the pieces of my life. If anyone should ever read these pages, remember I am only human (of the People of the Light; POL) and am as angry and biased as the rest of Split Humanity in the madhouse world in which we and our descendants are doomed to live. Today, I tackle the soul-ripping story of my family and our world.

It began on what was once known as July 13, 2025 – not a Friday, but still a mighty unlucky day for Humans. It was the watershed day that made the Black Death, 1918 Influenza, and COVID-19 look like blips in medical history. Everything changed that day at 11:40 am Eastern Stared Time; hell, they even changed the dating system to reclassify it as day 0, AfterFlare (AF). Everyone agrees on that designation, the POL and the Shadow People. In a bizarre twist, they call themselves the "Enlightened Ones." They are indeed what they are due to light - excessive light, as in a massive solar flare. They are also the most mutated, weak, mangled, cancer-stricken bunch of creatures you could ever imagine, like the zombie flicks BeforeFlare (BF).

The zombies at least were dead, so your 16-year old daughter wouldn't meet and fall in love with one on a particularly rebellious night, an AfterFlare Romeo and Juliet, except this love story might give you freaks for grandkids. So you do what any good father would do (and as required by law) and kill the mutant when you learn of the romance from your 5-year old son Freddie. So you earn your daughter's hatred and have to explain to Freddie why you killed Romeo (Tommy), actually, a smart, kind, and attractive Shadower. Little kids don't understand why the plague-carrying Shadowers must be avoided. Too young to understand why they must be feared and hated, hated because that's the only way your conscious will let you sleep after you kill them, as you must.

Give him time – Freddie's a bright kid and someday his mother and I will tell him that even though his sister Sally ran away in her distress and hatred of me, what I did saved her from Tommy and his kind. Hell, she began to hate all POL. And if I use profanity when writing of them, it's because they do live close to Hell, what with their underground cities, only creeping AboveWorld in the dark. They're more like vampires than zombies, non-biting vampires consigned to darkness, if they know what's good for them! When Freddie is old enough to understand the truth of the world, he'll stop hoping that his sister "will forgive me" and come back, that she didn't run away to another colony of POL, but to Shadowers - Tommy's family in the UnderWorld! I thought I raised her right – taught her right from wrong, good from evil, the warmth of light from the cold of shadows. Instead of sending her home, like any good POL would do, Tommy's parents blamed her for his death! Hah! Filthy slime! Just because I protected her from *their* son! If they would stop coming AboveWorld trying to refresh their gene pool, Tommy might still be alive. It's those filthy mutants we POL have to worry about. Can't get their defective, ever-shifting genes into *our* gene pool. That's why you got to kill them on sight, not let your kids run off with their warped offspring.

I worry about Freddie, though. Had to put bars on the windows and doors, seal the family in at night so he doesn't get any ideas about sneaking out to look for Sally, meeting some mutant kid running around in the dark and making friends. Don't want to have to kill his new "friend," too. Fred's been through too much already and I don't want him to think that Daddy is a murderer. Also, I have a hard time killing kids, even Shadowers. Just doesn't sit well, especially when they look normal, no matter what's lurking in their DNA, saliva, blood, and tears. Tears my heart out to kill them. Hell of it is, Tommy and others might stay well or their damned retroviruses hiding in our genes may not be infectious. With luck, Tommy's kids *could* have stayed healthy, but you never know and, somewhere down the line, his kids or grandkids will be born monsters. Tommy's sibs, if any survived infancy and childhood, might even be freaks. I don't know and didn't ask, just let Mr. Colt settle the problem.

Back to Freddie, once he's older, I doubt he'll tolerate those creatures any more than I do. He might even join Night Patrol when he comes of age in another 8 years - get even for his sister and make me proud. Me, I'm too weak-stomached to be a Patroller. Even killing Tommy made me sick for nearly a week, what with all of blood and the empty cavity where his lung and heart should have been. Hated to do it, but at least it took just one shot. He didn't suffer as much or long as me, in nightmares and

Sally's shrieking how much she hates me! Even years later, I still suffer when walking by her room in the morning, expecting her head to pop out from under the covers and ask what's for breakfast! I'll never hear her sweet voice again because Tommy's father didn't send her on home. While it was the right and only thing to do, killing Tommy that is, it still bothers me. Freddie, though, I hope that he's strong and man enough to be a Patroller and keep those filthy things UnderWorld. Besides, patrol duty is mighty respectable work.

But I digress. I want to also record what happened to humanity on Day 0, AF. Hard to keep from thinking about Sally and Tommy whenever I think how things could have been, without The Flare. Day 0 started out normal, like any other day in the former western Pennsylvania, west of the present Pittsburgh and east of Columbus and Cleveland Urban Centers. Sun was out, but it was threatening rain later. The Senate was in recess, so the wife and I went hiking. Plenty of ferns, birds, even some deer – beautiful creatures, not like their warped descendants. And trees, lots of them there – maple, oak, elm... been so long I hardly remember their names. We had a pear tree in the back and pears then were edible. Molly wanted a cherry tree, too. *Those* cherries were not only nutritional but tasted great to boot!

Anyhow, lots of shade on that trail on Day 0. Just Molly and me. Sally and Freddie were far in our futures.

Our friends from the bowling league used to kid us about the old TV show "Mike and Molly." Only Molly and I were in great shape. I hiked and biked cross-country then; of course, not now. Many of our dark-skinned bowling buddies made it only a few years, while the few surviving Light-skinners became Shadowers.

When The Flare occurred that morning, Molly and I got enough UV exposure for 20 lifetimes, even with those wonderful thick trees! And, as luck would have it, we were in a deep ravine with lots of rock outcrops over and about us. Still, Sun's first evil waves of radiation gave us well-done hands and faces. We wore long-sleeved shirts and pants since it gets cool in those mountains and protects against deer ticks and Lyme disease. There were mosquitoes and West Nile disease and a plant called poison ivy too, then. Turns out Sun, however, was and is the real threat, but mostly to those of us back then who got exposed, especially Light-skinners. Of course, Sun itself wasn't the problem - it was the incredible bursts of UV light from The Flare. Just about everything and everyone got dosed. Dark-skinners had had no idea the value of an extra dose of melanin! Back then, it was considered better to be a Light-skinner, if you can believe that!

Molly and I recovered from the skin burns. Our eyes, though, give us problems, even after cataract surgery. Was that in high demand for a while! (Fortunately, surgeons weren't outdoors when The Flare hit! Wouldn't want the blind operating on the blind!) All told, we were lucky! Ligher-skinners further south, especially on beaches or cruise ships, were dead men walking. And not for very long, either. The whites had purposefully exposed themselves to UV back then, believe it or not! And lay naked in "tanning booths!" Sounds too crazy to be true. Radiation from The Flare got them, or the burns. I'll never get those screams out of my head. And, later, most died. Since the hospitals were overrun, outpatient care was all most people could get. Since I had been a Senator, Molly and I got VIP treatment in outpatient care units in the old Pittsburgh. A couple of years later, when the US broke up into Urban Centers, I lost my privileges and was lucky to see any American Black or Indian doctors. Light-skinners have too hard a time staying healthy long enough to finish medical school.

Since everyone, POL and Shadowers, have different mutations, either directly from The Flare or inherited, health is an issue. Cancer, of course, but also blood, vision, and neurological diseases. Since folks with darkest skin suffered least from UV exposure, they're the healthiest and most intellectually stable. Dark-skinners don't generally get dementia-like problems until they reach their late sixties, while surviving Light-skinners begin to lose mental functions much earlier, especially those forced to spend much time outdoors during the day. Shadowers get hazard pay, but it doesn't seem like the risk is worth the benefits.

That's why some people have to be "encouraged" to take those jobs.

The POL must be, and stay, free of ERV. What ERV are and how they altered humanity beyond more than 1000 H bombs is a story for another day. For now, let's just say that any POL whose ERV become infectious are forever Shadowers and consigned to UnderWorld colonies. That's the only moral thing to do for us, and probably for them. More Sun exposure would only make things worse as infectious ERV are even more active when exposed to UV radiation.

Anyhow, many of the most critically ill who pulled through the first few months AfterFlare died of cancer in the next few years. They were lucky - those cursed got a heavy dose of UV and still survived, becoming the first Shadowers as their mutations became evident over the coming years or decades. Of course, the mutations themselves wouldn't have made them outcasts. It was their damned ERV popping out of their DNA and infecting other folks! Some other survivors had silent mutations in their more intimate parts that only became apparent after their children were born. Monsters – worse than monsters! Human monsters that were your children and could infect you and yours. They couldn't be allowed to survive! Many parents went mad, especially the women. Ultrasound and abortion clinics flourished as did mental health hospitals and, of course, morgues. Hard to find anyone dumb enough to dig graves, though. Too much Sun exposure, especially early AfterFlare. The incinerators fixed that up nicely.

That's about when the first Patrols began. Some parents just wouldn't take "proper" care of their kids even if they were infectious! Molly and I were spared that sorrow. World's upside-down when you're happier to have a miscarriage than a seemingly healthy, but infectious, baby. Molly had five miscarriages, but we were fortunate since the fetuses were deformed pretty badly. They weren't tested for infectious ERV, just incinerated, in case... No sense in exposing valuable docs to potentially infectious, mutant fetuses. The early Patrollers enforced the Infectious Agent Life Ban Act if parents wouldn't give up infected newborns for incineration.

The Ban, starting in central Europe among Light-skinners, spread to North American Urban Centers and then, the rest of the world. (Of course, Darker-skinners don't usually have infectious fetuses.) Soon afterwards, we required all fetuses to be tested prior to birth and aborted if they had any active ERV. The Patrollers then took over, incinerating infectious fetal material and quarantining mothers until they were found to be uninfected. If not, the chemical mixture provided a quick and easy death for the mothers, and safety for society. Light-skinners screamed "Discrimination!" rightly so, since most infectious fetuses and mothers are light-skinned, but the future of POL requires prompt elimination of those with active ERV. Civilization demands this sacrifice. Of course, some Lighter-skinners hide so their children are born in remote areas with the help of more dare-deviling midwives. Surviving infectious children are then smuggled to Shadowers. Shadowers welcome them - infuses their gene pool with "more normal" DNA. It's our kids, however, they really want as mates since Shadower DNA is mutating way too rapidly. So Patrollers really keep on their toes - not let Shadowers seduce our children by their "pity-me-I-live-underground" routine. Teenagers are rebellious and seek a "Cause." What's more romantic than secret lovers who only come AboveWorld at night and must dodge evil Patrollers? Grow up! Your lover may be infectious! Listen to your parents. Just like from the old Rogers and Hammerstein musical, *South Pacific*, you've got to be carefully taught, and taught young, before you're six, or seven, or eight. You had better hate all the people your relatives hate if you want to survive, and if you want POL to not perish. That came much later, though – at first, we tried, futilely, to live together.

May 27, 31 AF

Today's entry focuses on how to adapt to a world of energy and food scarcity. The first months were hard. The Flare knocked out most electronic devices the developed world relied on. The government, select agencies, the military, and some police in large urban centers still had power and could communicate and direct panicked citizens. They had hardened their electronics against electromagnetic surges from potential enemy attacks, not realizing our attacker would be Sun. As an elected official, I helped find power sources. It's amazing how inventive people can be when the chips are done, sometimes quite literally.

Americans don't hold the patent on ingenuity –poorer nations were used to limited resources. Dung became popular for heating and cooking for a while, even in North American Urban Centers and central Europe. In fact, with many animals dead or mutated too badly to thrive, dung = wealth. Who wanted to trade for cigarettes when rodent droppings kept you warm and allowed you the luxury of a hot meal to boot? Cycling became a major means of local transportation and bicycle delivery and messaging services boomed.

The power grids were eventually restored, but by then, people all over had made wind power and solar and nuclear energy work in economically sound manners, and our energy supply was better than ever. The biggest problems were the unexpected surges of wind and solar radiation as "smaller" flares, less than The Flare but still gigantic, continued for most of the decade. Of course, small flares affected winds and ocean currents, sea levels and precipitation, plus about every aspect of the environment was wildly see-sawing. Talk about climate change! And we puny humans thought we could really alter the climate! Nothing we did matched The Flare's havoc. One of the most problematic things was the unpredictability of the continuing flares. Until we learned when they would occur or Sun would calm down, we couldn't make any useful plans for normalization. Turns out, all prior predicative hard-copy models were good for was as a source of flammable material, similar to dung, but a non-sustainable fuel source, even if you had burned all academic works and governmental and regulatory reports. All of them - not worth horse droppings, just a former means of getting grants or putting fancy initials after your name. When it came to innovation, the people themselves, facing life or death, found what worked without needing environmental resources degrees.

The physicists, they're a different story. Their incomprehensible work with figures and formulas was the groundwork for the first useful solar activity models. That's probably why India is currently the world power. They're lucky enough to be Dark-skinners and great with numbers. The Japanese are major power contenders, too, but they're Light-skinners and spent too much time BeforeFlare on useless stuff, like "the internet" and "computer games." Back then, almost all of us spent lots of time "on-line" telling each other what clothes we wore and playing something called "Angry Birds" instead of studying something sensible like astrophysics! We had claimed to be "connected," but were actually just conceited and clueless about astronomical events around us. Having your nose stuck in an I-pod, or whatever, made you oblivious to the real world.

We ignored or misinterpreted climatic signs, claiming people were responsible for major changes! How vain could we get! While we did our fair share to kill off some species and push others to the brink of extinction, we ignored far more powerful solar activity. If only we had prepared: found ways to deflect Sun's wrath or built underground shelters to partially shield ourselves and some other forms of life! With solid planning, instead of playing imaginary "Angry Birds," we might've found ways to save some actual birds, and flowers, and trees, and bears! But we stuck with our erroneous models. We did see Sun as a power source, but drew a big smile on it, forgetting that too much energy is massively destructive. Global temperature trends should've given everyone a fair warning that something *big* was up, but people didn't look up high enough to see Sun doesn't wear a smiley face!

May 28, 31 AF

Today, I look at how The Flare changed, is changing, religious views. The mythical sun god Apollo was a jealous god and we didn't give him his due, claiming that the climate happenings were our doing. The Flare brought our attention back to Sun, though. It also brought some back to God, though many other people cursed Him. Some cursed God because their loved ones died, but more cursed God because their loved ones lived, but became Shadowers. Some people had clung to ancient prophecies and expected "End Times" with great disasters and death. Strangely, these Believers, with their doom-and-gloom predictions, got through the worst with the best attitude, even though they suffered most, with their running around trying to save people and animals or help infectious people. Strange they took it so well, or maybe not so strange... Believers still advocate for Shadowers. Won't join Patrollers. Say the Infectious Agent Life Ban is murder. I suspect some even meet with Shadowers in secret! They could get infected and infect sane people! That's why Believers are hated by so many people.

I admire Believers bravery and convictions, but who am I? Just a relatively healthy ex-Senator with a wife and one good child left. Things like Sun and its wrath, I understand. A loving Son of God, though, that's a bit of a stretch. My friend Jonathon tries to explain God's love in everything, but all I see is surrounded by the aura of the UV light of destruction and death. I keep listening to Jonathon, partially to appease him and partially because something in me wants to believe there is a loving Son and this is part of a larger plan. To be honest, though, I'm more than a little superstitious. I know Apollo was a myth, but what if God really exists? I want to be on His good side.

May 30, 31 AF

Today's topic is very basic: food. While I helped restore power, people themselves found unique, weird, improbable, and often useful solutions, so my major job was finding alternative food sources. I was very lucky. Many higher forms of animal life died off and crop plants were altered beyond recognition, forcing us to find new food solutions although with a vastly smaller human population to feed. I asked a botanist for help. Fortunately, plants have weird genetics. She started explaining about haploid and diploid and 1n and 2n, so I said "Whoa!" and asked for a translation for normal people. She told me that sometimes plants can survive changing their chromosomes' numbers and, in doing so, change their physical traits in ways that may make them better food sources. It's like humans going from pairs of chromosomes to sets of three or four and then being more useful. That happened with bread wheat. So we bred better bread wheat, corn, and beans – especially soy beans!

Now, we'd thought people can't possibly change *our* DNA to any great degree and survive to birth or, if surviving, would have major disorders. Boy, were we wrong! While we can't change our chromosomes' number like wheat, our DNA is much more flexible than suspected. We'd known about "jumping genes" and ERV (endogenous retroviruses) for decades without having a clue of how important they are or how much jumping a person's genes can do while staying healthy. Scholars simply had never seen massive numbers of people with "chromosomal alterations" or "activated" ERV. Of course, most people with altered chromosomes or activated ERV did die before birth or had horrible malformations, but not all. Not all. More on that later.

Besides new variants in our edible plant repertoire, we found other food sources – mutant insects and other icky things did quite well in adverse conditions. Less competition from other forms of life and The Flare's beneficial effects on their genes. Like other mass extinctions, survivors rapidly evolved to fill open niches. Roaches, of course, plus locusts adapted to new plant forms. We bred formerly unpalatable insects for size, nutritional value, and, in technologically advanced countries like India, South Africa, and Brazil, for their taste. Some Urban Centers in North America and southern Europe could import these delicacies, but most folks in blighted regions have enough problems just getting by and keeping minimal exposure to Sun. Amazing that our areas once controlled everything, with the majority population being whites! Dark-skinners in urban centers had miserable educational opportunities BeforeFlare. All that's changing now as evolution relentlessly replaces whites, ill-equipped to escape continued high levels of UV light, with better-adapted Dark-skinners as innovative methods improve education.

Food also came from another unexpected source. In the mornings, people in inhospitable desert regions globally found whitish coverings on surviving plant life. They first said, "What is that!?" Then some hungry people tried eating it. Surprisingly, it's an edible and very nourishing, rapidly growing fungus-like creature. It can't be stored up, but every morning, there it is again! People now just trust it'll continue appearing. Must be nice to trust you're cared for, food-wise, anyhow. We in Urban Centers of North America don't have this wonder fungus and probably wouldn't trust its daily return even if we did. We did try to farm it, but not even Indian scientists or South African crop technicians figured out how. It's beyond human comprehension, but not the grasp of hungry, grateful fingers. Not everyone is grateful, of course. Some want more meat. Migratory birds aren't good enough! They want lamb, wine, and olives, like BeforeFlare. Some people are never satisfied, even with full stomachs!

I shouldn't neglect the most popular meat source in Urban Centers of North America – rats. Rat farms multiplied rapidly since some mutated rats were larger, plump, and a better source of protein than cattle had been. Not too bad, once you get used to it. Tastes kind of like chicken. Algae also adapted well and are grown in large vats with edible bacteria.

People can adapt – have truly reliance on wind, solar, and nuclear power; new food sources; and new means of governance as people learned to do things better themselves than people we'd formerly relied on. Also, most importantly, vastly different social orders. The AfterFlare world belongs to Dark-skinners. The Flare led to the Great Split and the birth of Shadowers who must always be our enemies and kept in their place – UnderWorld, away from our children and our children's children forever.

June 2, 31 AF

Today, I'll explain how changes in DNA led to the Great Split and the changing social positions of Whites and Dark-skinners. One of my Indian biochemist friends tried very patiently to explain the genetics to me and this is my take on it. First, mutations in our DNA are bad; second, UV light can cause these mutations, and third, excessive UV light can cause ERVs, strange, ancient viruses hidden in everyone's DNA, to pop out of their chromosomal hiding places and become active, infectious viruses that cause diseases like cancer or cause more mutations. For any readers who wish to know more, here's a summary of my friend's explanation:

Early AfterFlare, we worked on food and Flare-related diseases and deaths. People, animals, and most plants in the northern- and southern-most areas, like Northern Europe and Canada, were just gone. Bacteria, other single-celled organisms, and some primitive plants did survive, though. Northern areas of the former US and Central

Europe were hit hard, too, especially Light-skinners. There was just too much UV exposure for almost all Whites. Dark-skinners in urban areas were some of the "winners" in all this, if you count living better than everyone else in your rapidly disintegrating country to be winning. Blacks and Latinos in urban America suddenly found themselves in the best physical condition in the country. As time went by, more and more of Light-skinner POLs sickened and died. North American Blacks and Latinos fortunate to have gotten a good education BeforeFlare became the leaders, along with the far less numerous people of Indian descent. Light-skinners had been the dominant force very early AfterFlare, but cancers began to take their toll on their survivors and hardly any were healthy enough to work or stay in school. Then worse diseases came, those due to newly-activated ERV (naERV).

BeforeFlare, few people other than microbiologists knew about the existence of ERVs. Everyone now knows that chromosomes are full of what was called "junk DNA." Biologists and biochemists then learned that parts of the "junk" were ERVs. Viruses, most people knew about, but not "retroviruses," even though HIV, the AIDS virus, is one. HIV's actually an "exogenous retrovirus" – comes from outside of human chromosomes. Many, many ERVs, however, are in our DNA normally.

How did ERVs get there and how do biologists know they're retroviruses trapped in our chromosomes? The

AIDS pandemic kick-started increased knowledge about ERVs. HIV DNA has on both ends unusual regions called LTRs. Other human and animal retroviruses have similar pairs of LTRs, so their presence is a pretty good clue that a retrovirus lurks (or lurked) in-between. Well, ERVs are flanked by the same type of LTRs. What's more, internal parts of ERVs contain genes very similar to those in HIV and other retroviruses, only mutated by exposure to small levels of UV light and other radiation over hundreds of thousands of years. A critical finding was that after HIV infects a human immune cell, it makes multiple copies of its genetic code and inserts them into the cell's chromosomes, staying there the rest of that cell's life, like HIV ERVs. When the cell divides, its new ENV copies go into the chromosomes of the two "daughter cells," then the daughter cells' progeny, and their progeny, and so on, with the ERVs kept within chromosomes of each succeeding cell generation.

Under certain circumstances, HIV ERVs become activated and they "pop out" of the chromosome, enter the cells' interior, and are transformed into HIV's normal form - fully active, infectious, deadly retroviruses! They then multiply rapidly, burst out of the cells, and infect new ones. In the new cells, HIV then repeats this process until it has destroyed most of the person's key immune cell type. Sounds like sci-fi, but it's true!

When scientists learned many of our chromosomes' ERVs look pretty similar to active retroviruses, they wondered if these ERV were also once regular retroviruses, like HIV, but didn't kill the cells whose chromosomes they "infected." To their amazement, microbiologists found that normal ERVs in human chromosomes could also pop out, make copies that live in the cells' interiors, and act like any other infectious retroviruses, infecting new cells. Fortunately, this happens extremely rarely! Scientists then linked several cancers and otherwise unexplained genetic problems to the activation of specific human ERVs. What's more, over millennia, ERVs made copies of themselves that jumped into new areas of chromosomes, thus "multiplying" tens of thousands of times in our chromosomes.

Now, if just one retrovirus infects one egg's chromosome, that person's children inherit it, just like their mother's other DNA. Say this goes on for thirty human generations. The former exogeneous retrovirus is now an ERV. Then something activates this ERV and it copies itself 15 times, with the copies jumping into other spots on chromosomes. Now there are 15 copies of that ERV. Throughout human history, such ERVs *have* been activated and copied themselves so that now much of our chromosomes are ERVs, the junk DNA, little genetic time bombs! Some ERVs have been caught in popping out and forming infectious, normal-type retroviruses that infect new cells.

Nobody really understands what sets off the process, even American Black, Brazilian, and South African geneticists, working on the problem since Year 1 AF. We knew even BeforeFlare that radiation, particularly UV light, can activate ERVs to pop out. Almost all these naERVs kill the cells they enter, but sometimes an infected cell becomes cancerous, multiplies, and spreads throughout the body, killing the person instead.

In the first six months AfterFlare, cancers began appearing in more and more people. Most cancers in the first five or so years were from UV light mutating people's genes. Then, doctors started seeing new human retroviruses in their patients' cells. Over the next several years, increasingly more, new retroviruses were found infecting people. Some of them, like U739, were only in blood, while others, like K265, were also in high levels in saliva and tears. Every new retrovirus was slightly different and caused a different disease. Some diseases were mild, but many were severe, causing cancer or deformities in fetuses and young children. Where were all these retroviruses coming from? The answer eventually became clear – they weren't new. They were the remnants of ancient retroviruses. They were our ERVs that popped out. Some just sickened and multiplied in their human host but some became infectious and were passed on to other people through blood, saliva, semen, or tears. They were our own army of "monsters within." Unfortunately, while starting in just one person, an infectious naERV can infect thousands of other people too.

June 4, 31 AF

Yesterday, I left off by explaining how infectious naERVs from one person can infect others. This ability of naERVs to spread to the noninfected people led to Split Humanity. Uninfecteds began to avoid Infecteds, treating them as the leper-like, plague-carriers that they were, and are. First, Infecteds were sent to Isolation Facilities, but some escaped, often aided by uninfected family members, friends, or soft-hearted, soft-headed members of human rights or religious groups. Human rights members and friends dropped by the wayside as they and their families became infected too. That brought them to their senses! Some families and religious groups, though, refused to see the light (literally!) and the harm they were doing with their misplaced love. Idealistic fools - putting everyone at risk by freeing Infecteds! And Infecteds themselves - you would think they would value society more than their insignificant freedom! The Isolation Facilities were bad, yes, but what could a bunch of plague-carrying freaks expect! We let them live, after all, although many Uninfecteds wanted to eliminate the threat by eliminating Infecteds.

I started out in favor of Isolation Facilities, then wised up and joined the growing movement to solve the problem firmly and finally. It appeared to be the best solution, only there were too many Infecteds to kill, *and* they selfishly fought for their lives. Worse, Uninfecteds started becoming infected as continued exposure to light triggered their own ERV time-bombs to pop out. Many originally supporting the final solution changed their tune then, afraid their own ERVs might pop and they themselves would be killed. Cowards!

The Ultimate Solution was a compromise, as weak-kneed members of the surviving government decided to really isolate Infecteds by consigning them to life in UnderWorld compounds built by Infecteds themselves. They were told this work would make them free and was safer than living in Isolation Facilities, but they actually were building their own large, living tombs that will forever cut them off from Sun and decent folks. All work was done to music from their own bands to give cheer to the proceedings and convince any remaining do-gooders that all was well and Infecteds were happy in their new homes. These Infecteds were the first of the Shadowers.

Shadowers must be kept apart – some naERVs may be acquired by merely breathing in wisps of their infectious breath while others are picked up by contact with blood, sweat, and tears, or sexually. The naERVs then act like HIV and its ilk – some just keep infecting cells, while others infect the cells' chromosomes, lying in wait, hoping to infect the person's sons, daughters, and contacts. With their potentially-infectious naERVs, Shadowers are dangerous to normal folks, and their offspring to all generations are dangerous, as well. That's why Shadowers must be kept apart, UnderWorld, forever.

It's really better for Shadowers to be kept in the dark, too. The Flare primed the pump, so everyone is now more prone to have their ERVs pop out if exposed to Sun. The most susceptible are Shadowers, but Light-skinners are also at much higher risk. Most Shadowers are Northern European or their descendants. Some Shadowers are also Dark-skinners, but they were the unlucky few with high exposure to Sun during The Flare or the smaller flares that followed. Yes, the healthiest, most robust people in the current age are darkest-skinned and, accordingly, they are the movers and shakers. After all, who would want to trust Light-skinners with responsible positions when they are more likely to have an ERV pop out? Light-skinners are viewed with suspicion, since some whose ERVs popped out try to hide their newly-acquired Infected status to avoid being sent to live with Shadowers, whose ranks they now joined by virtue (?) of their contagious naERVs. So Dark-skinners fear and shun Sun as a possible source of disease. And all POL, Dark- or Light-skinners, ban Shadowers.

It's a topsy-turvy world where dark is good, light is dangerous, Shadowers are forced UnderWorld, and even POL avoid undue exposure to Sun. All is fear, and UV rays in Sunlight is the ultimate source of the world's ills. Humanity traditionally equated goodness with light, loving the day and fearing terrors of dark and the night. The world of Shadowers is cold, with only artificial light. They long for real light and warmth of Sun but must be kept from them and from us. It is their destiny, as ours is to be vigilant and keep them in their UnderWorld compounds. Until a brave leader arises who will finally rid us of Shadowers and protect us from the ongoing threat of Sun exposure, we will never truly be free. I will raise Freddie right, for who knows, he might be the one for whom we hope...

TOGETHERNESS

Tales of romance and our connections with others.

2AM Call by Dawn E. Dagger

He Saved Her by Dani DeVendra

The Proposal by MKS Cooper

2AM Call

Dawn E. Dagger

THE PHONE BUZZED ON the nightstand beside me, filling the dark room with its blue light. I threw my arm over my eyes, waiting for it to go silent. The suddenness of the noise and light gave me a headache. To my chagrin, it continued buzzing.

Finally, I rolled over and grabbed the phone, trying to see the screen through squinted eyes. It was 2AM. Who on the forsaken Earth was calling me at this hour? The picture display was of a woman with long, brown hair.

"Why are you calling this late?" I asked as a biting greeting.

The woman's voice on the other end of the line was soft, heavy with melancholy, "I thought you'd be up. Sorry. I can go."

I struggled to sit up, grunting. "You've already woken me up. Why are you calling?"

There was silence on the other end for a long moment. I rubbed at my eyes, tempted just to hang up and go back to sleep. Finally, "I needed some company."

I groaned into my hand. "That's what bars are for." Though she didn't make any noise, I could hear the disappointment on her breath. That wasn't the response she wanted. "Why are you calling me? Why not call Hero boy?" I pushed myself out of bed and stumbled towards the hall. I needed a drink of water. She wasn't supposed to be calling me.

"I thought you'd be awake."

"So you said."

The night air of the hall was cold against my arms and torso. I moved into the bathroom, then got myself a cup of water from the tap. She said nothing as I gulped the glass of water down. I threw the cup haphazardly into the sink, grimacing at the loud clanging.

"I guess I just needed some company," she said reluctantly.

"Funny. Usually, you avoid my company." I moved back to my dark bedroom and climbed back into my warm bed.

She didn't hang up on me, as I assumed she would. She must have genuinely been lonely, to put up with my sour attitude.

I sighed, "Why don't you try to get more sleep, eh? I'll stay on the line. I'll be right here."

"Would you do that?" Her voice was meek, hope tinging at the edges.

"I just said it, didn't I?"

I heard shuffling on the other end of the phone. Once she was presumably comfortable, she murmured, "it's nice to have company. Y'know, a lot of times when I'm alone, something bad happens."

She was talking about me. As she should. As a Villain, it was my job to steal her away from the Hero.

The irony was not lost on me, and it made me chuckle. "Go to sleep, Civilian."

"Goodnight, Villain."

It wasn't long before her breathing changed from its melancholy shortness to deeper, quieter breathing. She had fallen asleep. My finger hovered over the button to hang up the call, but if I hung up, her phone would beep loudly. And that would wake her up.

So instead I set my phone back on my nightstand and resigned myself to suffering her loud breathing.

It wasn't long before I fell asleep too.

He Saved Her

Dani DeVendra

He found her on the brink of alcoholism.

She used it as a therapy to cope with the pain and suffering she had endured the past few years. She had put herself in bad situations, and let people take advantage of her until she became a hollow shell left with nothing to give, but her virtue to a man who had many before her. She always let the substance fill her body until it reached her soul, shattering it apart and trying to put the pieces back together with water instead of glue. Nothing helped, so, she drank the poison and reached for the love of a man that would never come.

She had hit the bottom. Her body was fully sunken under the water, no longer drowning from the demons, but submerged by them, dragged to the bottom of the ocean with no air supply. So she reached for another outlet, eventually meeting him. Golden eyes looked back out at her and she could see the purity in them, but she was too swallowed in herself to give him the time of day.

He was persistent and knew what he wanted, seeing a woman with a big heart succumbing to bad decisions cause she felt like she had no other choice. He confessed his love for her, and she thought she was not ready for it, but her heart had other plans, it fell faster than her brain could. And before she knew it, the honeymoon phase had begun.

He always stuck by her, from when she lost her grandparents to healing that inner child that so desperately needed freed. He accepted her crazy and scared. They had succeeded in finding what most people search for in life.

True love.

Beginning their life together, they never stopped at love. A ring was soon to follow only after a few months. And nine months after that, the crying of a baby began in a hospital room at 6:10 pm on a Tuesday where she lost herself again.

She became that hollow shell once more but for a different reason. She felt like she was a cicada, shedding its skin and leaving the dead one behind, but she was the part left behind. She reached for logic, and new fears and doubts rose in her mind. She felt like this could be the end, but she was not selfish enough to leave the world after creating such a small creature who depended on her to survive.

When he found out, he held her so tight that her eyeballs felt like they might explode. He never made her feel bad for the demons pulling her back into that ocean, but instead grabbed her hands and pulled her out after each storm every time. He had no idea how many times he had saved her. Once, twice... a hundred times. Because of that, you will always hear her say "I love you, K."

And she means it with her whole heart.

The Proposal

MKS Cooper

SHE HEARD ABE'S CAR even before he turned off the highway onto their winding, dusty driveway. He creaked open the door of the old vehicle and climbed out.

"We need a new muffler, Babe," she said.

"Do tell. Seems to me we need a new car. Supper ready?"

"Nah. Too hot to cook. I was thinkin' we might go for shrimp down at the pier. Ever since August hit us, it's like livin' in a giant sauna bath up here in the Panhandle."

Abe disappeared into their vintage trailer and emerged a few minutes later with two cold beers.

"Dang! It's like a oven in there!"

"I know. That's why I been outside all day."

They sat there, drinking their beers, enjoying the quiet around them. The trailer perched on a slope, surrounded by trees hung thick with Spanish Moss. Tall grass poked out of the sandy soil here and there. Dense underbrush advanced out of the woods, threatening to take over the yard. A shallow creek dribbled downhill, ending in a small pool at the edge of the woods.

She filled Abe in on her day. "I chopped out more brush this mornin' before it got too hot. Finally planted them petunias, too. The yard's startin' to look good. Oh. Dog got bit again. I saw him sniffin' at somethin' and before I could shoo him off, he went yelpin' into the woods with his tail tucked under."

Abe lifted his cap and combed his fingers through what was left of his faded red hair. "Lawz a'mercy," he sighed.

He stood up and looked around for Dog. The brown hound had showed up one day and stayed. He was the best dog they ever had, except he couldn't mind his own business, always investigating one darn thing or another. They thought maybe someone would show up to claim him, so they just called him Dog. Now, he'd been with them over a year, and the name had stuck.

"After he run off, I found him down by the creek with his nose in the water. I coaxed him back home, but he got under the porch, won't come out. Hurt his pride more'n anything, I think. I saw where the snake got him, just nicked his nose and made it swell up some. He'll be okay."

Abe sat back down with another beer, looking at her through his cigarette smoke. He considered her a pretty lady and was proud to be with her now for over two years. Every once in a while he wondered how he'd got so lucky to have her put up with an old redneck like him.

She'd had a rough time growing up, and some more tough times with guys that treated her bad. But she'd come through it all loving to laugh and have fun. Sometimes, though, she'd get down way low and cry a lot. After a while she'd be herself again and things would go smooth for a long spell.

Abe didn't think much about it during her good times, but now, looking at her sitting there so peaceful, he wished he could do something to keep her like that. It was hard on him, when she cried.

The sound of tires broke in on his thoughts.

"Oh Law, here comes Crawford."

She looked up at the truck slowing to a stop in the driveway. She loved Crawford to pieces, but all day her mind kept seeing that crispy fried shrimp, piled in a basket with French fries and coleslaw on the side, with her sitting there talking to Abe while someone else cooked their meal for a change.

Crawford stumbled on the first step, his work boot landing in the new petunia bed next to the porch.

"Go he'p him up, Abe. I'll get some supper goin'."

The men followed the smell of fresh-perked coffee into the kitchen and sat down to watch the magic that happened every time she pulled out the frying pan. In no time, the smell of frying chicken filled the room as potatoes were browning in the big black skillet. A plate appeared on the table, filled with vegetables picked that morning from the garden.

Crawford eyed the thick slices of tomatoes and cucumbers, the skinny green onions and shiny red radishes. When she turned her back to check on the crisping chicken, he snitched a piece of cucumber.

"I saw that, Crawford," she said, without turning to look at him, and they laughed as he tried to eat it without crunching.

They ate everything, down to the last buttered biscuit, including a second pot of coffee and apple pie left over from the day before.

Abe turned off the television set and walked Crawford out to his truck after the late news.

"Thanks for stoppin' by, Crawford. You be okay drivin'?"

"Yeah. I been drunk so many years this old truck learned the way home by itself a long time ago. Sorry I stayed this late, Abe. She makes a body feel s'welcome, it's hard to leave. There's never been anyone makes me feel s'good about myself as she does. You better marry her, Abe, or I'm gonna ask her."

"You know what, Crawford? She's so fond of you, she'd prob'ly say yes. Now git on home, before you find yourself in trouble, you old coot."

Abe stood by the couch for a minute, watching her sleep, then bent over to kiss her hair.

"Wake up, Babe. Time for bed."

"Is Crawford still here?"

"Nah. He's half-way home by now. It rained. Cooled off some. Wanna sit out for a bit?"

"Sure. I'll get a towel and wipe off the chairs."

They propped their feet up on the picnic table bench. Abe chuckled.

"What's so funny?" she asked.

"Crawford says he's gonna marry you if I don't. Would you?"

"You askin' would I marry Crawford, or you askin' would I marry you?"

"I guess I'm askin' would you marry me."

"I would if you asked me."

"I'm askin'."

"Yes. I'll marry you, Abe."

They sat silent in the dark until Abe started chuckling again.

"That was good shrimp we had for supper. Let's go back to the pier tomorrow night and have some more."

"Oh, I don't know. I'm kinda tired of eatin' out. Let's stay home and I'll fry up a mess of chicken."

When they stopped laughing, Abe said, "You know what? I don't tell you enough, but I love you."

"I love you, too. I been thinkin', why don't we get married right here in the yard? There'd be room enough for everybody. We could roast a pig and pick corn and tomatoes from the garden. . ."

He leaned over the arm of his chair and kissed her.

"Only one thing I want to say tonight. We goin' to find you the prettiest dress anybody ever wore to a weddin'. The rest of it we'll figure out in mornin'. You ready for bed?"

"I am. You s'pose Crawford made it home in one piece?"

"Better have. He's gonna be my best man."

The screen door squeaked shut behind them as Abe laughed again.

"Sure hope he don't drop your ring in the petunias."

THE UNKNOWN

Vampires, ghosts, and legends... stories that contain the supernatural and the unknown.

A Quiet Dance by Dawn E. Dagger

BloodRose by Alexxa Burton

The Search for Lake Atagahi by Dani DeVendra

A Quiet Dance

Dawn E. Dagger

CAT PAWS ACROSS GROUND, whispering across the dusty floorboards, shuffling footsteps. Against the window pane silver raindrops tap softly. The trees that crowd the house reach out, tapping against the glass, asking to join them. The moon shines bright despite the rain. The moonlight dances in the raindrops that slip down the windows, creating soft, dancing shadows.

The whispering feet turn then move a little faster. There are two pairs of footsteps, though someone just listening would not have known it. One spins the other, and the footsteps, though different, create a perfect rhythm. The drapes rustle as they waltz past. The flowers in the vase upon the stand turn in their container. The phonograph crackles as the record spins. The lamp in the corner is off, but the moonlight provides enough light for them.

Somewhere above them a door slams. The floorboards creak as the heavy figure moves. The water pipes rattle. But none of this bothers them. The house is haunted. And so what? The haunting creature never bothers them. The worst it does is move the furniture some days. A baby begins to cry.

But it doesn't matter. All that matters is the one in their arms, their captivating partner in dance.

They dance to the music from the phonograph. Thunder rolls across the sky and the room is illuminated by a crack of lightning. Not even the storm can stop their perfectly timed dance. They are not bothered by the crying baby or the phantom which barks from the drawing room, nor the stumbling, shadowy creature that flicks on the lights in the rooms upstairs.

They have one another, cold hands pressed together in their timeless dance.

The ghostly couple spins through the night, one with the moonlight and the rhythm of the raindrops, until the sun comes up and washes them away.

BloodRose

The Making and The Lake Chamber

My name is Kateel and I am a vampire.

How many books on these shelves start that way? How many of my kind have felt the need to put pen to paper to tell their immortal story to immortalize themselves in a different way?

I know. Vampires aren't real. But really? Are you certain? I'm not some ancient vampire. I grew up in modern times with modern conveniences. I owned a cell phone. I drove a car. I read popular stories. I knew vampires to be a thing of fiction, but never really believed it.

You know how you walk down the same street every day but still have no idea what shops line its sides? The existence of my kind, and many others... it's a bit like that. Humans, at least those who go about their lives expecting nothing unusual, simply don't notice us. Simply don't register bits of oddness at the edge of their awareness. So, we live together: side-by-side and yet apart.

As a human, I was obsessed with vampires. I searched legends and folklore. I found clues to the world I sought. And painfully slowly, I became aware.

I was in love with the vampiric nature, and the idea of immortality, enthralled with it. As I learned more, I found my way through the darkness of the mortal shadows and into the world of eternal night. I was stepping through a door into a story, about to have a grand adventure.

That door was an old, dilapidated door to a vampire bar. You'd think it was just any abandoned building if you walked by, windows boarded over and dark, door threatening to fall off its hinges. I too thought it was abandoned until one night I noticed smoke coming from the chimney.

The night I was turned was not the first night I dared to enter that place. I had been there several times. Enough that a few of the patrons grudgingly recognized me. There was nothing particular about this night to make me think it would be unlike any previous.

I sat in a highbacked chair looking into the fire. I had an exaggerated vision of what I looked like sitting here, long red hair cascading over my shoulders in perfect waves, black cloak thrown behind me, copper-colored skirt pooled around me like liquid metal. I imagined the firelight playing in my green eyes as I stared into it, and watched it flicker across my skin. To live in a flame... wild and free, where nothing could stop you.

I imagined myself the perfect immortal creature sitting there...

An ancient vampire walked in radiating a hot crackle of power that danced across my skin and into my soul. It was like nothing I'd ever felt before. Almost like staring a wolf in the eyes, knowing at any moment it would dart in for the kill, and yet, standing your ground. The fear of it, the excitement of it, was intoxicating.

He strutted, there could be no other word for it, and took a seat at the bar. He sat facing away from me. He simply sat, still as stone, tall and proud as a mountain. I let my eyes rest on his broad shoulders, considering the possibilities.

I came up behind him, a hand tracing along his shoulders before taking the seat beside him, then reaching over and taking a swallow of his drink. It was confident and bold. It may have been stupid. Or perhaps it worked in my favor. I was about to stand and walk away, trying to entice the hunter to hunt, when he turned to look right at me, his storm-blue eyes meeting mine. I stared back.

Eventually he rose and took my hand. I could feel him playing at the edges of my mind, examining me as a predator might examine a creature they suspected was prey, but whose behavior was confusing. I shook my head, smiled, and stood, letting him lead me out the door.

We walked down the street, me half a pace behind, letting him think the situation was under his control.

I turned off abruptly at an alley. It took him three paces before he realized I wasn't beside him. He looked at me, eyes narrowed, thoughts churning through his brain.

I smiled and shrugged saying "Well come find out." with my eyes. And he did, this time him following me. Was it the best choice to have this predator, with whom I'd yet to exchange a single word, at my back? Probably not, but fortune favors the bold.

I led him out of the city to a secluded spot at the edge of the river before I stopped.

"The prey has stopped running?" His voice was like liquid chocolate.

"Or was never prey in the first place."

He took my shoulders, spinning me roughly to face him. "You, my lovely, are indeed prey, no matter how confident you are or how you may surprise me."

"I may turn out to be food but I'm not prey."

"I don't know whether to be frustrated or amused. I don't like it." He took me by the throat and bared his teeth.

I laughed.

He blinked in shock then tightened his grip.

I continued to laugh. Almost maniacally now. "Bite me then. Drink. And turn me."

He froze. I took his wrist and removed his hand from my throat, well aware that he let me. "Looks like you've chosen to be amused."

His face was emotionless, but in his eyes, I could see his mind spinning.

"My name is Kateel."

He stood there, all stormy eyed and brooding.

"Simply standing there not communicating isn't productive in the slightest."

"Garrett." He growled out the word.

"Now we're getting somewhere."

His eyes bored into mine. I felt him again at the edges of my consciousness. I didn't let him in.

"What do you want from me?"

"I told you what I want." My voice never wavered.

"You want me to turn you," he said slowly. "What makes you think I want you following me around for the rest of eternity?"

"I won't be following you around."

"A fledgling alone? You'd be lucky to last a week."

"Wouldn't that be my problem?"

"I don't understand you. I thought you were looking for death, or reckless excitement, the thrill of being with a vampire. But to be spawned and abandoned, that's more than foolish, that's crazy." He went silent for a long moment, looking deep into my eyes. "Just maybe you're the right kind of crazy. I shouldn't care. I don't know why I care. There is something about you. I felt it even before I saw your face."

"You're right. You shouldn't care. But I can do this." I smiled. "I'm just that kind of crazy."

He took me around the waist and pulled me in.

"I'm not afraid."

"I know you're not," he whispered. I could tell even this confused him. Fangs grazed my throat almost playfully. My heart pounded. His teeth broke my flesh. I could hear my heartbeat, feel the blood moving through my veins, and his pull on it.

What can I say that a hundred other stories haven't? You know how this works, the spawning of a vampire. He drank from me, then gave me his blood. At some point I lost consciousness. When I woke, I was alone with his words echoing in my mind. Words of survival he must have imparted while I was unconscious. You know the warnings. Sun, fire, beheading, stake to the heart.

The sun was close to rising. I don't know how I knew, but I did. I took refuge in the earth itself, digging into the soft ground of the bank of the river. Something I would not recommend. It made a mess of my hair.

Did I ever see Garret again? Of course I did. There were many nights he and I walked together. But I'm not ready to tell those stories, not yet.

Several things became apparent soon after spawning. The first, that I was the right kind of crazy to make being a lone fledgling work. I wouldn't be here now if I hadn't been.

The second, as a human I'd always been able to read people well. To be able to do and say the right things to get any outcome I wanted. Almost as if I was inside their minds. As it turns out, I was. I'd thought I was just observant, or had good instincts. And I had the uncanny ability to keep people, and creatures, out of my mind, to make myself practically unreadable to them.

Those were fairly low-level empathic skills. As a vampire I am a hundred times more capable. I can now do things people would laugh you out of the room for if you said you could.

As Garrett's vampire blood worked its magic on me, I found I could read peoples' thoughts if I focused, and directly influence them if I focused more. People I was familiar with, I could locate wherever they were just by listening for their minds. That's how I was always able to find Garrett, a trick even he couldn't replicate.

These are helpful things for a vampire or so you might think, but it proved to be a double edged sword. Humans naturally suppress many of their thoughts, fears, anxieties, depression, regrets. They do their best to hide those things where they can't feel them. But when faced with an overwhelming fear, all those other fears break free of their confinement.

When feeding, I become connected, immersed in a victim's thoughts and emotions. If my food is terrified, all that fear and sadness comes crashing into me, swiftly becoming overwhelming. Even a willing victim often loses control of their innermost emotions when faced with the reality of dying. Being hit with all the fear and pain in a human mind can incapacitate me, much like a human having a panic attack. I feel weak and pathetic admitting to succumbing to human emotions that aren't my own. I am a predator, and prey shouldn't have such power over me. I have found very few ways around this problem, even now. In those early days, as I traveled alone, most of the options I now know were unavailable to me. Many nights, more than not, I went hungry.

There's a fear in being constantly hungry and unable to feed oneself. The fear and hunger became my nightly companions. And when I did give in, when my vampire instincts drove me to feed, it did not go well.

I was close to this point one night as I walked through some woods, far from that place I first stepped into this world. The ground gave gently under my steps and the leaves rustled in the trees with a life of their own.

Slowly a feeling of panic gripped me. This was more than just the fear of being hungry. Something was following me. And it wasn't alive. I spun around and something darted into the shadows.

I thought of going back to the vampire bar where I'd started my night hoping this thing wouldn't follow me there. But it was blocking the path. I crouched low to the ground, growling. I saw a pair of glowing blue eyes in the trees. I leapt toward them but the creature darted away, unscathed by my attack. I pounced again, throwing my body toward the creature. Something ice cold passed through my fingers for an instant, then was gone, and I was facedown on the ground. I looked up. The figure with the blue eyes was ahead of me. I snarled savagely, tensing for another attack, then tilted my head, listening.

The creature was whimpering, scared. I realized how small it was. I knelt down among the leaves and beckoned to it, my eyes softening.

"It's alright. I won't hurt you."

The creature slowly stepped, or rather floated, into the moonlight. It, he, was in the form of a young boy. His form shimmered, translucent blue against the trees.

"What are you?" I asked.

"I'm a ghost. My name's Caleb." His voice trembled.

"I'm Kateel. How old are you?"

"I'm nine. I've been nine for twelve years."

"Why are you following me?"

"I saw you in the vampire bar. I didn't recognize you."

"I don't remember seeing you."

"You wouldn't've. I was invisdible. You looked sad. How's come?"

"Why were you invisible?"

"I'm a'scared of the blood drinkers."

"Then why play there?"

"My friends do, and I don't want to be alone. I think you don't want to be alone either."

"Where are your friends now?"

"They went home to the caves. But I wanted to meet you."

"Ghosts live in caves?"

"No, just me. They're werewolves. I stay there too though. Lady Ravyn is kinda nice but Lord Greywolf is pretty scary. Lady Ravyn takes in people who are lost and helps them. Are you lost? I could show you the way. There's a lot of not nice things in these woods."

"I can find my own way."

"You don't believe that. I can see things like that. You should come with me. I can teach you all my favorite games. I know you want to come, you don't want to be alone. Lady Ravyn is a blood drinker too, she can help you. At least come stay the day. You don't want to get caught outside when the sun comes up."

I slowly nodded agreement and reached to ruffle the child's hair but my hand passed through the top of his head. I tried to suppress a grimace at the icy chill that shot up my arm.

Caleb shrugged his little shoulders. "You'll get used to that."

He led me to the mouth of a cave near a lake. "It will be dark. It's a long way down, but it's really pretty. You can see in the lake."

"In the lake?"

He didn't answer, just entered the cave. The air cooled as we moved deeper into the earth. I heard scrabbling on the rocks around us. My eyes darted from side-to-side but my vision was filled with things I couldn't quite see. A dim glow began to soften the darkness.

"Are you ready to see in the lake?"

I nodded and followed him around a sharp bend. The room shimmered with the shifting blue glow of light shining and reflecting through the water. We were under the lake. It had a glass bottom that formed the walls and ceiling of the chamber. I stared up in amazement. It was beautiful. Fish swam around above me. It was like I was immersed in another world.

"I told you it was pretty," Caleb whispered.

A woman sat on a stone step surrounded by children, a wolf cub sprawled on her lap. Her eyes were yellow, like a raven's, as she locked her gaze to mine.

She stood, her gown flowing around her ankles and black hair falling to her waist. She approached me, the grace of her steps as elegant as her features. There was something liquid about her movements. She reached out and her fingertips touched my temple, touching her mind to mine, a feather light touch, barely there, never threatening to break my defenses but the woman's touch still sent a shock through me. This creature was not like any vampire I'd yet met. I didn't know what she was. I'd never seen anything like her before.

"She's starving." Ravyn's voice was a melodic alto. "Bring one from the catacombs."

A man dressed all in black disappeared silently down a corridor.

We stood there, eyes locked, unspeaking. It couldn't have been more than a few minutes before the silent man came back guiding another into the chamber. He was an old man, sickly looking, every rib visible on his shirtless torso. There wasn't the slightest hint of fear or even awareness in his cloudy eyes.

Lady Ravyn guided him by the back of the neck till he stood in front of me. She leaned in and whispered in my ear, "Feed child, his mind is gone, all that's left is the body." Then she drew back, leaving his fate to me.

I put my hand on the side of his neck, drawing him to me. He allowed his body to mold to mine as if touch was the only thing he recognized. I bit him, bracing myself against the mental assault but it didn't come. There was only quiet emptiness as I fed.

When I'd emptied him, I let the body fall to the floor leaving it for the silent man. I looked at Lady Ravyn, unsure what to say. Should I thank her for the meal?

"You will stay here until you can sort out your affliction. Feed on the mindless ones in the catacombs. It is my hope once you are properly and consistently fed you will be able to manage the minds of your victims more easily." It wasn't a question but a statement.

I nodded.

"Caleb can show you to a room. I'm certain he is eager to explain this place."

Caleb was smiling up at me hopefully. I smiled back, a lopsided smile that hid my fangs, amused with his innocent exuberance. I followed him, his hand reaching back for me as if he could pull me along.

Once we were alone in the corridor, he began to talk incessantly. "Lady Ravyn is a witch who was turned into a werewolf but then bitten by a vampire too so she's a little bit of everything. Some of the other children are like her too, well without the witch part, but some are just one or the other. I'm the only ghost though. Well, there may be more in the catacombs but no kid ghosts. I hope you like it here. It's a really nice place. It'll be nice to have a new friend." He kept talking until after the sun had risen for the day and I had fallen asleep.

I woke up the next evening in a small room. I looked around. I hadn't the night before, with Caleb talking at me about everything and nothing. The room was nondescript, raw stone walls and floor, a small table with a candle set on it, and the simple coffin I was sitting up in. It wasn't a room meant to be a home, just a place to stay.

I remained sitting there, unsure what to do, what I was expected to do. I knew this place was home to the pack of werewolves and the few vampires Lady Ravyn considered her family and that she took in all manner of creatures in need of help. It struck me as odd. I'd had no encounters with werewolves before but it was my general impression wolves and vampires typically didn't get along, much less reside together. Being around other vampires gave me pause too. Aside from public vampire bars which people typically treated as neutral ground, I had mostly steered clear of other blood drinkers in the time since my making. Aside from Garrett.

A blue form stuck its small head through the door. Through. The door. It was Caleb of course.

"You're awake! I've been waiting for you to wake up!" He floated the rest of his little body through the wood of the door and into the room. "Do you want to come out into the lake chamber and play I Spy with me? All the werewolf kids went out and left me here. It's a full moon and they said no ghosts allowed." He pouted.

I agreed, simply to take the sad look off his face, and before I knew it the two of us were looking up through the glass into the lake "spying" interesting fish and different colored rocks. We were the only ones there with the wolves presumably having gone out to shift. I had no guess where the other vampires might be but I was relieved by their absence.

It was perhaps midnight before Lady Ravyn appeared. She was alone. I got the sense this woman was very rarely alone. Part of me envied that. She took one look at me and said, "Why haven't you fed yet?"

I was caught off guard. I was hungry, yes, but I'd fed the night before. I could hardly remember the last time I'd fed two nights in a row. The idea hadn't even occurred to me.

"Caleb, show her to the catacombs. No, you don't have to go in if you don't want to. Kateel, you should be feeding nightly and you are welcome to do so. Any mortal you find here is yours for the taking. And if you wish to go out and hunt, you are welcome to as well. I expect you to not let yourself go hungry."

"Thank you, Lady Ravyn. You are most generous."

"This place is here to help those who need it and I endeavor to provide all that is necessary for such. You are welcome to all that is here."

Caleb was already... on his feet?... ready to show me to the catacombs but I stayed where I was, watching Lady Ravyn take a seat where I'd first seen her the night before as a small parade of werewolf cubs entered the chamber, bloody from their hunt above. One by one, she cleaned the blood off each of them. She was so tender with them, as if they were truly her children.

I followed Caleb down into the maze of tunnels until we reached a heavy stone door.

"I don't wanna go in. It's scary down there."

"You don't have to come if its scary."

"I'll see you tomorrow, Kateel. We can play more games."

He floated off and I pushed open the heavy door not knowing what I'd find. It was cooler down here, almost cold, and again, completely dark. I heard small sounds of shuffling and breathing, but nothing made any attempt to approach me or even seemed aware of my presence. I could sense there were more than just humans but what those other things might be I wasn't sure. Possibly even things I'd never conceived of and had no names for. Slowly, I made my way deeper into the darkness until I came across a human sitting quietly, cross legged, on the ground. This one would do.

I swiftly drained him? Her? I didn't even look. And just like the night before there was only peaceful silence. Again, I wondered what I was supposed to do now. Leave the body here? Dispose of it somewhere? I had no idea where, if so. I opted to leave it there and return again to my room where I simply sat alone in quiet reflection. After so long, it was quite an odd sensation to not be hungry.

Throughout my time there, I continued to keep mostly to myself, spending the hours in my room or down in the catacombs. I found I quite enjoyed just sitting down there in the peaceful, quiet darkness. My favorite place was still that first chamber under the lake but aside from the early evening and early morning it was usually too occupied to be comfortable.

The werewolves set me on edge. They were loud and raucous, constantly posturing and squabbling amongst themselves. The few vampires at the compound shunned me for the most part. I was an unknown factor, and though I was clearly there for a reason, I was still different than them. My psychic abilities exceeded what most vampires could do, and they were understandably wary. I clearly came from a very old, very strong bloodline, but they couldn't tell which one and I wasn't sharing.

Caleb was my only companion.

After a week I woke to the sound of claws scrabbling down the corridor outside my room. I opened the door to a pack of werewolves, mostly cubs but a few adults, racing past.

"Greywolf's back! Greywolf's back!" rose out of the cacophony.

The mythical Lord Greywolf had returned from wherever his wanderings had taken him. Hesitantly, I trailed behind the wolves to the lake chamber. I looked for Caleb's blue glow but didn't see it. He'd always said Greywolf scared him. Maybe he was hiding, or invisible somewhere.

Greywolf's power radiated from him to fill the room just as Garrett's had, but unlike Garrett, what emanated from Lord Greywolf made my skin crawl.

I'm not certain what it was but he made me extremely uneasy, more so than any of the other vampires or wolves that inhabited this place. He maintained a half wolf appearance. In the remainder of the time I was there, I never once saw him in either a human or full wolf form. A preference perhaps? With the level of power that dripped off him, it certainly wasn't a shortcoming.

Lady Ravyn was clearly pleased to see him as they stood arm in arm, her looking up at him. It seemed the whole pack had congregated, and for the first time was calm, not fighting among themselves, as they filled the chamber.

I stayed in the back, watching the reunion, listening as he spoke a few sentences to each wolf. I could hear most of it and could feel the emotions rising in the room. They liked Greywolf and respected him, but also feared him and I could see why.

Eventually his eyes settled on me. He turned to Ravyn and asked "Another stray?" He kept his voice low but I could still hear him.

"Her name is Kateel. She needs help and sanctuary."

"She smells like a problem," he growled.

"Kateel has been nothing but respectful."

"Those she comes from, those she's attached to, are not likely to be."

"She is on her own," Ravyn interrupted before he could go further.

Could he smell Garrett's bloodline on me?

Lady Ravyn gestured me out of the chamber with her eyes, and I went back to my room.

The remainder of my time there, I kept to myself even more than I had before, rarely leaving my room or the catacombs. I only ventured to the lake chamber when it was empty of others, aside from Caleb of course.

The beginning of the fourth week, I sat in the lake chamber watching the last rays of the sun disappear in the western sky. It offered a glimpse into a different world, almost swallowed me into it. I liked this early time when the colors of the world I'd forsaken shown through the lake into my world below. I watched the refracted golds, reds, and blues dance across the stone floor. It gave me a chance to think.

I closed my eyes and let my mind fill with visions of the dawn. The soft pinks and oranges blending into the blue of the morning I would never see again. Imagining the catfish and other nocturnal animals above taking refuge in their hideaways as the diurnal fish came out in search of food.

I felt a hand on my shoulder. I opened my eyes and was re engulfed by the night. I saw only darkness now through the bottom of the lake.

Lady Ravyn stood there, her hand resting on my shoulder. She looked at me with deep sad eyes, those eyes that were always so kind and knew so much.

"You're not happy here," she said.

"You've provided a wonderful sanctuary here, Lady Ravyn. I am grateful for it. How could I not be happy?"

"You make your own happiness child. Nothing I or anyone else can give you can change that.

I looked at her wondering what she was telling me. There was always more to her words.

"You will always be welcome here, but you must go where your heart leads you. You have regained your strength, now you must light your own candle and find your own way home." She turned her back to me, heading deeper into the caves, gown swirling gently around her feet.

I knew she would never directly ask me to leave, but she had deemed it time for me to do so. I sat there a long time just looking at the water while the night passed. I didn't want to leave but I didn't want to stay either. And in her own way, Lady Ravyn had told me she understood that. I sat there and watched the moon rise, watched the catfish scavenge for food. I knew there was one thing I had to do before I left. I made my way through now-familiar tunnels to the woods above.

The forest was alive with the sounds of the night. The path which weeks ago had eluded me now jumped out in the moonlight. The same woods, the same path, the same little boy, very different ending.

I sat against a tree in the same spot where I'd scared him so badly that first night. The night was half over when I felt that cold, tingly, not quite there touch on my arm.

"Hello Caleb."

"What's going on Kateel? You never come out here alone."

"I'm going away Caleb, maybe for a long time."

"Are you going with Lady Ravyn? Sometimes she goes away when Lord Greywolf is here."

"No Caleb. I'm going by myself."

"Are you coming back?"

"I don't know, I don't know what's going to happen next."

"Let me go with you Kateel."

"You can't do that Caleb, your home is here."

"I don't want to never see you again. You're my friend."

I smiled. "I'm glad I'm your friend. And as long as we're friends, always know, someday you will see me again." I rose to my feet and headed down the path into the woods toward whatever waited for me.

The Search for Lake Atagahi

Dani DeVendra

Gatlinburg, Tennessee, named after the most hated man in town around 1854: Radford Gatlin.

One of the homes to the beautiful Smokey Mountains and a legend of a lake hidden from human eyes.

One of the stories tells of a young Cherokee man spending his days fasting and praying in the mountains. Due to the state of his heart, and the purity of his intentions, Lake Atagahi, or known as the Enchanted Lake, shows itself to him. The young man then marks it with a pile of stones so he will always be able to find it. Not long after his discovery, the Cherokee Nation had a horrible winter and most were starving. The young man decided to return to Atagahi seeking food for his family. He took his bow and fired at a bear, watching it fall into the water and reemerging unharmed. The bear then speaks to the young man, telling him he had betrayed the lake, and then the young man was attacked by an angry hoard of animals.

My group's mission is to find this lake and prove the legend to be right or wrong. We have been studying the Smokey Mountains for weeks leading up to this trip. Preparation was key. Knowing how to survive in these mountains is the only thing that will keep us alive. Knowing what is lurking out there prepares us for any bears, rattlesnakes, foxes, etc.

The Smokey Mountains are huge, ranging from the borders of Tennessee and North Carolina, one of the main entrances being in Gatlinburg. So, that is where we are heading. I always wanted to visit there, it is a dream come true for me. I grab my backpack from the floor of my apartment. The clinking from inside echoes off the silent walls, making it seem more empty. Since the group and I travel a lot, I have not fully settled into my apartment yet and still have boxes piled up in a corner of my living room.

I met the group in high school, only a year ago. We were all taking geography when one of the girls in our group mentioned places she would love to explore. We decided from that day on we would meet and become urban explorers for fun after graduation, then eventually made our way down the list of places we wanted to see.

We started with exploring abandoned homes around us in our hometown. Next were other cities around us. And now, we decided to explore Atagahi after stumbling across the legend in an abandoned home. After doing our research, today is the day we head to Tennessee and begin our adventure to the hidden lake.

I walk out the door to my apartment and down the stairs to the running van waiting outside.

Mitch, the potential leader of the group, is sitting on the driver's side, taping on the steering wheel and bobbing his head to the music playing. Liv, Mitch's girlfriend, sits in the passenger seat scrolling on her phone, her other arm resting on the widow, holding her head up. The last person in the car is Shane, he's head banging to the music playing and I watch him and Mitch start to sing together, getting in a groove. Shane lifts his head and stops suddenly at the sight of me. My heart jolts and I awkwardly wave to him. He rolls the window down and the sun reflects in his golden eyes, making them shimmer. "C'mon, Sunshine, we don't have all day!" He shouts, motioning me to get inside.

I chuckle at the nickname and nervously reach for the door handle. I sit beside Shane and buckle up my seat belt. "Two more to pick up and we will be on the way to Tennessee. Who's excited?!" Mitch shouts and we all cheer.

Twenty minutes later we have Emmy and Luca, brother and sister, in the third row arguing about something the other said.

Four hours and a long ride later, we hit Gatlinburg at an extremely slow rate. It's packed, and people line the sidewalks. I look around and see tons of tourist attractions and restaurants. People rush through the streets to get to their destination.

"We need to find a place to park, eat, and then camp," Liv says, rolling her eyes at the crowd.

"Wait, I thought you had to start fasting tonight?" Luca asks while holding a water bottle up.

"It was never officially discussed. I assumed we would start tomorrow." Mitch shrugs and looks over to an annoyed Liv.

"I need one last cheeseburger in me before I hike up that trail," she scoffs and turns toward me to back her up.

"I could go for a burger," I say with a smile.

After fighting traffic, we finally find a spot to park and choose the first place we see to eat.

After we all finish eating, Shane pulls out a map from his pocket with the Appalachian Trail highlighted. "This is where we are," he points and traces his finger down the yellow marked line, "And this is where the trail ends. It will take about four days to get to North Carolina on foot and four hours of driving. Emmy and Luca will meet us in the van in North Carolina. No matter what we find or not, this is an adventure!"

We all cheer and high-five each other.

It was going to be a long four days.

Day One

We passed multiple people on the first day. We were so excited and full of energy. Our backpacks are becoming heavier by the minute. We make camp at nightfall, the trees around us swallowing us up in the darkness. The sounds of rustling leaves and breaking branches startle us all as we stay in the mountains for the first time.

"You know, I heard this trail is haunted," Mitch announces after lights out.

"Shut up!" Liv and I groan together. We were scared, afraid of what the night could bring us.

All four of us huddled together in a small tent, awaiting any danger that came for us, but none did.

Day Two

The four of us struggled to sleep last night. After Mitch's announcement, I tossed and turned most of the night. The cold air had crept up into our tent, the four of us shivering, and we did not pack enough warm blankets. To find Atagahi you need to begin fasting, so it was water from here on out. The second thing on the checklist was to pray to the Gods and have pure intentions in your heart. So we began silently praying every two hours to the Gods that Lake Atagahi would appear to us, allowing us to see its beauty.

We hiked for several hours today. My body shook from exhaustion and my legs buckled as we inched closer and closer to the end of our destination, but we were still two days out. We set camp right off the trail, careful to not walk too far away from it and become trapped in these mountains forever. The sun begins setting and darkness hovers over the tree lines, awaiting its turn. My pulse races as we listen to Mitch talking about ghost stories he read up on before our trip. Goosebumps raise on my arms when he mentions creatures up in the trees that you should never make eye contact with.

"Alright Mitch, knock it off. You're scaring the girls," Shane rolls his eyes at the overenthusiastic Mitch and his stories.

He was right though, I was terrified.

Day Three

Shane and I stayed up most of the night after hearing the stories Mitch rambled on about. As much as I love adventure, I do not get thrilled out of being scared to death. Every sound we heard in the darkness last night had our heads turning and our pulse racing. We heard growling in the distance and I nearly jumped out of my skin into

Shane's arms. We have started to see fewer people now, most of them deciding a couple of hours is all they needed, but not us.

We so desperately wanted to see Atagahi, its enchanting waters that have been said to heal the wounds of animals. There was not much else to go on from but a few legends passed down from generations. "In one of the stories they say that the lake was marked with a pile of stone, so to-morrow keep your eyes out for anything that could look like that," I manage to say through my pants. The others notice and pull me aside to take a break. With no food for two days, only water, and hardly any sleep, my body was ready to give out.

I remove my backpack and set it to the side, it's been weighing my body down and I had little energy as is.

"Here," Shane says, holding out my water bottle. It was the last one I had brought. Thankfully tomorrow this will all be over. As much as I loved adventure, hiking was my least favorite thing to do.

I take a sip from the bottle, the water has turned warm in the weather and I sigh in disappointment. I could use a cold drink right now. And probably a shower. The four of us sit in silence for five minutes before Mitch looks down at his watch.

"Alright guys, time to pray." He removes his backpack, setting it on the dusty ground, and hits his knees. The rest of us follow suit and repeat the prayer in our heads.

The wind kicks up, knocking down the backpacks that we had set on the ground. We stare at each other with wide eyes. The trees were too tall to have a wind so strong.

"Tell me that was a sign that we are getting closer?" Liv asks with excitement.

"I think so!" Shane shouts.

It was the step that we needed for our excitement to come back. I scramble to my feet, grabbing my things that were toppled over from the wind. "Okay guys, I'm ready, let's go!"

By the end of the night, the four of us are exhausted and soaked in sweat. My clothes cling to me and I feel dirty and damp. I watch the boys slowly set the tent up while Liv and I gather wood for tonight's fire. In ten minutes, the sun will set and the darkness will once again swallow us, the trees around us giving cover but putting us in danger too.

There was no talk of ghost stories tonight, just hope for what tomorrow will bring.

We are only miles from what could be such a huge discovery, and as excited as I was to witness it, I was more excited to eat some greasy fries.

"I'm calling it a night," I announce after Liv finishes a story about an abandoned house she exploded as a kid. I felt better going to sleep if everyone else was awake.

"Me too. See you guys in there," Shane waves goodnight and scrambles to his feet.

Waves of anxiety dance through my body with the thought of us being alone together. "It's early, are you sure you're ready to sleep?" I ask him once we are settled inside the tent.

"No, but someone needs to protect you." He smirks and dims the lantern, the light slowly dies down until it's almost out. "Aren't you worried the tree people will get you while we are all at the fire having fun?"

I swat at him, his comment causing goosebumps to form on my arms. "Not funny," I grumble at him.

He chuckles and shifts his body to face me. "As long as I'm here, you're safe from the monsters."

Day Four

Today's excitement between us was like we were on our way to winning the lottery, that our numbers matched the ones on the T.V. and we were getting a million bucks. We started this morning by looking at the map to see where we were and where the two borders meet. If Shane's map was right, we'd be there in less than twenty minutes. That news made us extra perky and the excitement buzzed on. I finally decided to take in the scenery since I was no longer worried about how much longer till we got there.

I turned my head in every direction, trees spread for miles and the Appalachian Trail thinned, only marked with a small bit of warm grass. No one had been out here for weeks, and if they were, there wasn't enough of them to make much of a mark on the overgrown grass. A few feet ahead, beautiful purple and pink flowers were sprouted across the ground. Bees buzzed and birds were chirping overhead. Excitement bubbled in my chest.

"Do you guys hear that?" I ask with a smile. The three of them stop and try to listen to what I heard. "In one of the legends, it says that Atagahi can be known by the singing of birds! Lots of them!" My mind rushes with excitement. We were so close I could taste it. I could smell it!

"Look around for a pile of rocks. We have to be close," Liv perks up, scanning the ground around us.

Excitingly, the four of us go separate ways to search for a pile of rocks. My eyes scan all the ground around me and when I see nothing, I move to another part of the mountain and search there. Hope blooms in my chest as the singing of the birds becomes louder. The flowers bloom excessively in this area and there's movement around me. A bunny hops out of a bush and I yelp from surprise. It looks at me, its eyes scared and body stilled.

"I'm not going to hurt you," I assure, moving slowly toward it. It senses my movements and quickly leaps away, hiding in another bush. I don't know why, but I follow the bunny like I'm *Alice in Wonderland*. I watch the bunny hop fast and stop to turn toward me, looking like it's making sure I follow.

After the fifth time the bunny stops and waits for me, I'm sure I have lost my mind from exhaustion and starvation. The bunny stops moving and hops onto a medium-sized stack of rocks. My heart jolts and I smile wide. The pile of rocks is in front of me.

"I found it!" I holler, hoping I do not get myself lost in these woods. I hear shuffling around me, too excited to pay attention to what direction it's coming from. My feet move forward and I stop myself, I want the others there with me to see it, but the shuffling stops and everything goes quiet. "Guys?" I shout, my heart thudding at the silence.

It's like the earth stopped turning and the birds got put on pause. It had to be a sign that we had found it.

I move forward without thinking and push past overgrown bushes, tree branches clawing at my skin, and twigs catching my feet, feeling like they are trying to hold me back. I yank out of the grip and move forward. Above the overgrown plants, I see a clearing and just like someone hits a play button, the world begins to move again. The singing of the birds is loud and beautiful. I sigh before pushing past everything, this is it! We have found Lake Atagahi. I close my eyes before making my last step out into the clearing. I hesitate to open my eyes for a moment, taking it all in before seeing it for myself. This was the place. The lake was here and I was about to see it for myself. With a deep breath, I open my eyes and take in the sight.

Nothing.

Nothing but a dry mudflat.

THE FAITH

Stories that embrace religion, and rejoice in Jesus Christ. Stories of comfort, triumph, and purpose.

The Centurion by Bill Reid

The Bloody Man by Bill Reid

The Tale of the Country Cat by Donna J. Bunner

The Fable of the Christmas Spider by MKS Cooper

The Centurion

Bill Reid

Striding along the dusty, pebble-strewn hillside, the Centurion kept a watchful eye on his men as they prepared for the task ahead.

This Centurion was no ordinary officer; his leadership and bravery had become a legend among the legion.

From humble beginnings in a poor section of Rome, he joined the Roman Legion at a young age, rose up through the ranks, and became a fierce fighter. With a 'sixth sense for military strategy', he was able to mold the soldiers under his command into the 'most elite fighting force' in the Roman Army.

The most important attribute any officer can have is the ability to take care of his men. The centurion took this responsibility to heart. He led by example, and made sure his soldiers had equipment, clothing, training, and as fresh of food as possible. This was done to keep them fit for battle, but also fit for life after their military service. As with any army through time, even elite forces were not immune to mundane or grizzly tasks, such as this day. For this was the day of crucifixion.

As the Centurion, making his final inspection of the of the area, he was also checking the position of the sun. Execution was always set for the third hour of the day. He was certain the time was right, but he could see no one.

All of a sudden, two soldiers came running up the hillside, yelling. They were the soldiers he had sent down earlier to look for the soldiers and prisoners. "They are here! They are here!"

The Centurion hurried to the crest of the hill, and he could see why they were late. Instead of two condemned prisoners, there were three. But his most trying concern was the large, howling mob following behind the prisoners. As the procession gained ground, the Centurion could see the soldiers were stumbling backwards, trying to hold back the horde. These soldiers were Garrison Troops of Jerusalem, under the command of Pontius Pilate.

The Centurion turned his attention to the badly beaten prisoner at the front. He slowly realized who the man was. *Is this not Jesus of Nazareth?* He asked himself. *The one who called himself the Christ, the Messiah?*

As the rabble grew closer, he could hear the chanting, *"Crucify him! Crucify him! Crucify him!"*

As the Centurion and his troops travelled through the country side, they had encountered Jesus from a distance a couple of times, when he was teaching throngs of believers. What had changed, or what had Jesus done, to be put to death in this manner? The Centurion and his men were encamped outside the city walls. So, they were not privy to the previous day and night's events that lead to the enraged mob.

The Centurion turned to his second in command, ordering him to prepare the prisoners for execution. A dark-skinned man helped bear Jesus and his cross over the last few feet. The Centurion passed them and saw just how beaten Jesus was. A rush of guilt passed through him. How had the man not died on the road to the hill called "The Place of the Skull"?

After the exchange of the prisoners with the Garrison Captain, a new order from Pontius Pilate was handed over to the Centurion. It stated that to hasten their death, the men's legs were to be broken. This act was to appease the Jewish leaders. The bodies would be taken down before the preparation for the Sabbath, which began the next day.

After the Garrison troops left, the Centurion's main concern was the howling throng. This was not the kind of mob he was expecting, but then again, a mob was a mob. He scanned the crowd, looking for the main instigators. He spotted a few chief priests near the front of the mob. At the rear were some Jewish leaders, yelling for crucifixion the loudest. The Centurion and his troops had been transferred to Jerusalem the month before, rumors had been spreading of a great uprising during the Passover Celebration. The Centurion and his men were the ones to quell any riot.

While the Centurion thought about his next plan of action, a shrill, razor-thin scream cut through his brain like a sharp knife through a melon. The scream came from the condemned men as the soldiers nailed each one to their individual cross. The cross were driven into the prepared holes in the ground. The screams startled the mob, and a few faint-hearted ran back down the slope. After a moment or two of silence, the mob started back with all of their frenzy.

On a hunch, that morning, the Centurion had added a few more men to his command, for an emergency. They were arranged in a semi-circle in front of the crosses.

A few of the bold ones, including one or two of the chief priests, ran up to the line of soldiers. The Jewish leaders laughed and scoffed. "He was so good at helping others," they said. "Let's see him save himself if he is really God's Chosen One, the Messiah."

The crowd picked up the chant, "come down from the cross and save yourself if you are the Christ!" More laughter and scoffing.

The Centurion watched Jesus, who was praying to God the Father. "Forgive these people, for they know not what they've done."

By the sixth hour, darkness fell across the land. The light of the sun was gone, and in the distance a large storm started to form. Black clouds made the sky even darker, and great lightning flashes blinded them.

Around the ninth hour, Jesus cried out to God, "why have you forsaken me?"

A soldier rushed to him with a sponge soaked in sour wine. He offered it to him to drink, to ease the pain. But Jesus, with his last ounce of strength, shouted "it is finished!" and his body collapsed against the cross.

With his words, a large flash of lightning cracked through the sky and crashed to the ground. The Earth seemed to split in half. It was so intense that most of the horde, including all of the High Priests, made a hasty retreat.

Time slipped away, and the Centurion ordered his men to break the legs of the prisoners. When they came to Jesus, they realized he was already dead. A soldier thrust a spear into the side of Jesus, and blood and water flowed out of the wound.

Before the prisoners could be taken down, the Centurion had one more duty to perform: he had to verify they were dead. He checked both of the thieves, then faced Jesus. Though he had a mortal wound, the Centurion thrust his sword into the man's side. Blood poured down the blade, onto his hand and arm. As the blood travelled across his shoulder and down his other arm, the Centurion was transformed. He felt no anguish or tension from the events of the day, only warmth, compassion, and love. He had never felt this way, even as a young boy. It was like two, strong arms engulfing him.

He looked up to see if Jesus was still hanging there. He was. In a strong voice, the Centurion asked, "Can you not see that this man was truly the son of God?"

At that moment, another intense flash of lightning hit the Earth. What was left of the rabble, including a few blood thirsty hangers-on, hastily fled back down the slope. The only ones left were the wailing women who had stayed at the fringe of the mob, including the mother of Jesus. The Centurion fell to his knees and cried profusely. He did not feel the hard rain, only the warmth and love.

His men were amazed.

Out of the gloom came four men, two elders and two younger men. They had an order from Pontius Pilate to release the body of Jesus to them for burial. The Centurion later learned that the two elders were Joseph of Arimathea and Nicodemus, both secret disciples.

The body of Jesus was taken down and the four men wrapped it in new linen. Then they slowly started down the slope, out of sight.

After the two thieves were taken down, the Centurion knew what he had to do. He gave his helmet and sword to his second-in-command. He would be a follower of THE CHRIST.

THE END?

... NO!

.... IT IS THE END OF THE BEGINNING!

The Bloody Man

Bill Reid

THE BATTERED AND BLOODY man fell on his knees right in front of me. As he hit the cobblestone street, blood gushed from the wounds on his body. Only vicious criminals would getting such a beating. What crime did this man commit, to be beaten within an inch of his life? Our eyes met and, although his body is broken, his spirit was not. No anguish in his eyes, only compassion and love.

He looked deeply into my soul, for a only few moments, but it seemed like an eternity.

My father grabbed the back of my tunic to life me up and out of the way of the soldiers' feet. They proceeded to push the bloody man along the narrow way. Soldiers were trying to keep order as the crush of the crowd was greater than before. Looking down, I noticed some blood had collected in a small crease in the cobblestones. It wasn't blood from the wound on my hand, but from the man.

The blood was dark red, but a translucent light emitted from the pool. The light had the same sparkle as the sun reflecting on a calm body of water.

I knew I had to recover the blood. But how? I pulled a clean cloth from underneath my tunic to soak up the blood. I wanted to be a physician, so I needed to study anything that affected the body. From my pack I took out a wooden bowl we had purchased at the market earlier that day.

I squeezed the blood from the cloth into the bowl. It was still dark red and pure as before, but I needed more. The crowd, which had turned into more of a mob, was still yelling and cursing, but they had moved down the street. The soldiers were trying to keep order, but to no avail. Along the street men and women were crying in a low, mourningful wail.

I hurried down the street, looking for another pool of blood. By then, the mob was out of sight. I spied another small pool in a crevice up ahead. As I was soaking up the blood, by father came running up behind me.

He grabbed my tunic. "Son, we must flee from the city at once! Look up ahead." In the distance, a storm was brewing. "We must leave now," he shouted.

As I stood, huge, black clouds were forming. Bright yellow lightning flashes split the dark sky. Powerful gales of wind blew through the streets.

My fathered gathered up our goods and pressed me away from the storm. I hurriedly squeezed the blood from the cloth into my bowl and covered it up, hoping not to spill any on the hurried way home. Fortunately, home was away from the story. Finally, we were out of the city, hurrying along the dark, dirt road that would take us home.

In all the excitement of the day, I forgot about the cut on my hand. The wound was caused by moving the crates around the market. To my wonder, the cut on my hand had completely disappeared. As I examined my hand, I could not find any scar or evidence that the cut had ever been there!

Late in the evening, we finally reached out village, exhausted. My hunger was overpowering, so I ate some bread and honey. Before going to bed I poured the blood I collected into a vase, put a cover over it, and cleaned out the bowl.

The next morning, after the morning chores, we had our meal. Father told Mother all the events of the previous day. After our meal I retreated to my room and retrieved the vase of blood. I poured a drop or two into my hand. The liquid was still dark red, but the glow that I had seen when I collected it seemed to have faded.

Later that same morning, I overheard my neighbors talking to my father and mother about the events they had witnessed the day before. The neighbors, along with the other villagers, had not been participants of the howling mob, but innocent bystanders caught up in the fury of the day. After the Bloody Man was taken out of the city, he was executed by those soldiers. This was only a few hours after the crowd had passed us. Once the Bloody Man died that the storm broke with all of its fury, scattering the mob in all directions. They sought shelter from the storm's might, and most had to stay overnight so were just then returning to their respective villages.

Four days had passed since that eventful day. As was the custom, in the evenings my father and a group of older men would gather around our fire pit for fellowship. From time to time, my father would allow me to sit in on these meetings. The order of the day for me was just sit, listen, and learn.

That discussion was different, though. It was about the execution of the Bloody Man.

Some said they had heard of this man from various travelers coming into the village. Other people in the surrounding countryside also heard of the man and his many followers, but were unwilling to repeat the stories until then. They relayed stories of this man: healing the sick, the lame, the blind, and even lepers. My mind raced. Was this man's blood responsible for healing the cut on my hand? What kind of power did they man have? Did the authorities execute him because they were in fear of his power?

Once the meeting concluded, my father walked me to bed and wished me good night. But I couldn't sleep. I could only think of the man and the blood in the vase beside my bed. I promised myself that the next day I would see if all the stories I had heard were true.

In the early morning I retrieved the vase, hoping none of the blood had dried up. When I looked inside I saw there was still a large amount of liquid, easily enough for my test. My cousin lived down the road with a large boil on his leg. His mother had tried every potion she could find, but none were able to heal his leg. I grabbed the vase and hurried over to my cousin's house. Once there, it took no persuading for my aunt to allow me to use the blood. She was willing to try anything.

I poured the rest of the blood from the vase in a bowl. I dipped a cloth into the bowl, then dabbed at the boil, making sure to cover all of the wound with it. I wrapped his leg in a clean bandage, saying, "all we can do now is wait."

I waited three days, then went back to my cousin's house to check on his progress. After removing the wrapping, we were all surprised to find the wound had completely healed!

In the following days, there were rumors coming from the city concerned the 'dead man.' Many stories claimed that the 'dead man' had been sighted in parts of the city with his followers. The thoughts plagued me, until I decided I had to learn more about the man who healed me and my cousin. I must seek out his followers.

I must learn about this man that they called THE CHRIST.

The end....
... is far from over.

The Tale of the Country Cat

"GOOD MORNING PASTOR," MILLIE greeted Pastor Ankrum as she walked inside the church.

"Good morning Millie. Beautiful day to be in church this Sunday morning isn't it?" Pastor Ankrum asked.

Millie nodded and shook the Pastor's hand. Millie felt a hand on her shoulder, and it was her Aunt Hilda. She loved her Aunt Hilda, but she never liked to be too close as she could always smell chewing tobacco on her breath. Millie wondered why she had to chew her tobacco (or as she called it "tobackey") so loudly . Her Aunt Hilda was her favorite of all of her Grandma's sisters. She was the only sister left now on her beloved Owl Hill.

Since her Grandma passed away the year before, Aunt Hilda had been trying to step in and fill her place as much she could. She had finally got off them cigarettes, thanks to Grandma. Aunt Hilda had a high-pitch singing voice that was always beautiful to hear while the congregation was singing the hymns.

Millie heard tiny footsteps running. Suddenly, Lillibeth greeted her and give her a hug. Millie loved having Lillibeth in her Sunday School class.She was the cutest 5 year old in her class. Millie knew she couldn't play favorites, but with the strawberry blonde hair and big, blue eyes, how could she not be a favorite?

That day, she had the cutest red polka dot dress on. It really brought out the blue of her eyes. "Hi, Lillibeth. You look so pretty this morning," Millie said.

"Are you ready for Sunday School, Ms. Millie?" The little girl asked.

"I'm so sorry sweetie. This is my Sunday off. I'll be your teacher next week."

"Oh rats. I love Mrs. Jacobs, but I love you more", said Lillibeth.

Sally, Lillibeth's Mother came and stood beside her daughter, saying, "Come now child. Leave Millie alone. Let's get to class."

"She's not a bother at all Sally," Millie intervened on behalf of her favorite student.

Lillibeth smiled and asked, "Do you have any candy for me Ms. Millie?"

"Lillibeth, for goodness sakes. Come on. Let's get to class," Sally said, exasperated.

"Just a minute," Millie said, opening her purse. She pulled out Lillibeth's favorite: mini *M&Ms*. As Millie handed Lillibeth the small container of *M&Ms*, Lillibeth smiled.

Sally looked at her with a stern face and asked, "What do you say to Ms. Millie?"

Lillibeth looked up at Millie, smiled, and said, "Thank you Ms. Millie. Now you know why you're my favorite teacher!"

Millie couldn't help but laugh.

Grandpa Mehl started the service by welcoming everyone from the pulpit. Millie was so proud of him. He had been asked to become the new Sunday School Superintendent, since Mr. Chambers passed away. Her Grandfather loved this little country church with all his heart, and it truly showed through his smile and the kindness the congregation received from him.

As Grandpa Mehl continued to take prayer requests, Millie looked over and see a couple of new faces she has never seen before. Some of the congregation were her aunts, uncles, and cousins, but she wasn't sure who this couple was. They seemed to enjoy the banjos that cousin

Larry and Donald played, while Eliza sang old hymns out of the red hymn books.

Millie noticed that the pew the couple sat at didn't have a hymn book sitting in the slot in front of them. She was going to make sure that one was placed there after service.

After Larry and Donald were done singing and strumming "When We All Get To Heaven," Grandpa Mehl started playing "Amazing Grace" on his fiddle. Millie always loved to hear Grandpa's fiddle. It always brought tears to eyes, along with the smile on her face. Millie happened to glance over at the couple, and noticed tears streaming down the gentleman's face.

Grandpa's music always touched everyone in some way. Never a service went by that Grandpa didn't play. The country folks are spoiled by his playing.

When Grandpa was done, he placed his fiddle in the beautiful, purple felt case.

Preacher Ankrum walked up onto the pulpit to begin preaching. He asked the congregation to turn in their Bibles to Genesis 1:1. He started reading the scripture when all the sudden there were gasps from the congregation.

A tortoise shell cat came jumping through the window! It was a beautiful cat, with black and orange and brown markings on it. The cat walked in and sat on the piano bench. She just sat there, as if she wanted to hear Preacher Ankrum too.

Brother Ralph stood up to pick up the cat, and put it outside, when Brother Ankrum said, "No. No. Leave it there. It must need to hear about Jesus too."

Laughter was heard throughout the congregation. Pastor Ankrum preached about God's creation: it took 6 days, and He rested on the 7th. The pastor looked over at the cat and then back out to the congregation, saying, "So, I have a little question for you all to see if you'ins have been listening. Including you-" He looked back at the cat, and the cat meowed as if to say "Amen".

The congregation laughed.

"Here's my question for you all: what day did God create animals like this beautiful creature here?" Pastor Ankrum asked.

"I'm gonna guess. It was the second!" Sister Potter yelled out.

"Nope. That's when He created the sky", said Pastor Ankrum.

"Weren't you listening Mama? It was the fifth day," said Loretta.

"That's right, Loretta," said Pastor Ankrum.

Sister Potter gave Loretta a stern look as some members of the congregation snickered. Pastor Ankrum finished his sermon and gave the altar call. He asked if anyone needed prayer, and the gentleman that Millie has been wondering about walked up for prayer. As Brother Ankrum went to pray with the gentleman, the cat jumped off the piano bench and went beside the gentleman. The cat just sat there beside the gentleman, like it was helping him pray.

When the prayer was finished, the cat jumped back up on the piano bench and just sat there. Pastor Ankrum asked if anyone else needed prayer. No one else came forward, so Pastor Ankrum concluded the service by asking the congregation to repeat the phrase, "God is good all the time and all the time God is good."

Pastor then went on to say, "Please stay today as we are having our Summer Picnic. If you didn't bring anything, please stay anyway. Also, just a reminder that Revival starts this week. I'll be continuing the Creation topic, 7 o'clock each night. Now, let's pray over our food. Father, we thank you for the food that we are about to receive. May it bless our minds and bodies. Bless the hands that prepared it and bless this time of fellowship. We ask you in Jesus name we pray, Amen".

"Now let's eat!" yelled Mr. Cummings from the congregation.

Millie walked towards the edge of pew, towards the center aisle, to greet the couple. She reached the end of the pew, and the couple stood up. "Good morning," she said. "My name is Millie."

The gentleman extended his hand to Millie. "Nice to meet you Millie. My name is Jonathan, and this is my sister Monica."

Monica said, "Hi. Nice to meet you," as she shook Millie's hand.

"I hope you both can stay for the picnic. We usually do a picnic every other Sunday after church for fellowship- and to have fun too. We usually have horseshoes and frisbee matches too. Some times Grandpa will play his fiddle and we'll have a hoe down," Millie explained.

"We would love to stay, since we are new to the area and all," said Jonathan.

Before Millie could reply, Pastor Ankrum came up to introduce himself to the couple. "Well, howdy folks. I'm Pastor Ankrum. So nice to have you here this morning!" Millie introduced the couple. "Well nice to meet you both. Welcome." He shook each of their hands in turn. "Welcome. Are you you'ins from around here?"

"We just moved here a month ago. My Grandma passed away and left the property to me. I'm going to be going to *West Virginia University* in a few weeks. Monica is just with me for the summer. She'll be going back to Ohio soon to finish up her teaching assignment and hopes to move back here soon after that," Jonathon said. "What's the story with the cat?"

"She's beautiful", Monica said.

"Well. We don't know. This is her first visit," said Pastor Ankrum.

"Just like us," Jonathan said with a chuckle.

"You all are welcome to stay and eat with us. We have plenty. The women around here sure do know how to cook."

"Yes, please follow me," said Millie.

Jonathan and Monica followed Millie outside to the small picnic area. The three walked over to the back of the line. The line moved slowly as the table was filled with choices of potato salad, macaroni salad, pizza, ham slices with buns for sandwiches, baked beans, chicken, creamed corn, green beans, and coleslaw. Jonathan saw another table of desserts, along with a canister of coffee and another canister of tea. *Kool-Aid* sat in cups on the table.

Mrs. Ankrum walked past and said, "Please make yourself at home. We're all country folk around here."

As soon as Millie, Jonathan, and Monica were done at the food table, they found the nearest table to sit at.

As Jonathan set down his plate, he asked Millie, "What would you like to drink?"

"*Kool-Aid* is just fine," Millie answered.

As Jonathan walked away, Lillibeth came running over to Millie and said, "Hi, Ms. Millie. Did you get enough to eat?".

"Well, not yet. We just sat down to eat," Millie answered.

Jonathan was walking back to the table when Lillibeth blurted out, "Who are you? You're kinda cute."

Sally came rushing over, chiding, "Land sakes child. Let these people eat in peace. Come on Lillibeth." She put her arm around Lillibeth's waist to guide her away from the table. "Goodbye, everyone."

Millie grinned and turned to Jonathan and Monica and asked, "So where do you live?"

"We live at my grandmother's old house, off of Deavers Fork. I remember coming here every summer as a kid and spending the summer with her. I never thought when she passed she would leave *me* the house when she had fourteen other grandkids. Where do you live?"

"I live around the corner from here- in a white house. I live with my Grandpa Mehl, the one who played the violin. My grandma passed several years ago so it's just me and him ever since."

"Awww. I bet you miss your Grandma," Monica said.

"I do, everyday, but especially when we do our church picnics. Everyone for sure misses her rhubarb cherry pie."

Just then Grandpa Mehl walked over to the table and said, "Well, I hope you alls are getting enough to eat."

"Yes. We did. Thank you."

"Good to hear it. So glad you visited with us this morning. Don't be strangers around here. You're welcome anytime."

Millie stood up to throw her plate away and asked, "Are you going to play horseshoes Grandpa?"

"Well only if my new friends are up for a challenge."

Jonathan laughed and said, "I haven't played horseshoes in years. I think not since our last family reunion."

"Well, come on then! Show me what you got."

As Jonathan left with Grandpa, Monica told Millie that she could help clean up.

Neighbors of Owl Hill always loved Revival Week, and the summertime, because they knew that Grandpa would play his violin with the church doors left open. The doors were left open to let in the breeze off the hills and cool off the building. Some set chairs outside as they thought the roof would fall on them if they entered the building. Pastor would always tell everyone to 'come as you are' and that 'Christ loves you where you are at now in your life.'

Grandpa was grateful that his violin playing touched so many- inside and outside the building.

The next morning Grandpa walked to the church to change the sign to announce revival, and to start cleaning the building before church service started. Millie hung the clothes out to dry on the outside clothesline while Grandpa was gone. Millie she wondered if Jonathan and Monica would come to service and if the beautiful orange and black cat would reappear.

'Be the person your cat thinks you are' the church sign read.

The looks on the congregation as each person read the sign was comical. Some gave stern looks while others laughed.

Grandpa Mehl went up to the front and got his violin out of its case. There was a flash in the window. It was the cat from the day before, visiting again!

He went to the same spot on the piano bench and looked as if it was ready to listen to Grandpa play. "Look. There's a cat. Is that the same one everyone was talking about?" Lillibeth asked. "I missed it, since I was in Junior Church after Sunday School."

"Yes. It is the same cat," her mother said.

"Isn't she beautiful?" asked Millie.

"I want to pet her," said Lillibeth.

"Come with me." Millie took Lillibeth's hand and walked her to the stage. As Millie walked towards the cat, Grandpa Mehl began playing 'When We All Get To Heaven" on his fiddle. The cat sat still, its eyes closed, as if admiring the music. Millie pet the cat's back, and it immediately started to purr and rubbed her head against Millie's hand.

"Awww. It's so sweet," Lillibeth said. She started to scratch its ear, and it rubbed its head against her hand. "I think it likes us. I wish we could take it home with us."

"What? Take it home with ya? Then who would come visit us again through the window?" Grandpa asked, still playing, walking over.

The cat jumped down and started doing figure 8's around Grandpa's legs.

"Grandpa, I think he is thanking you for your fiddle playing," Millie joked.

Grandpa stopped playing and stooped down to pet the cat. The cat looked up at him with squinty eyes, just purring and purring.

"You're a sweet thing aren't ya?"

Other members of the congregation came inside the church. As Grandpa went to each person to greet them, the cat followed him. When he would start talking, the cat would sit by his feet and listen. Everywhere Grandpa went, the cat went.

"I think Grandpa has a new friend," Millie said.

After Pastor Ankrum preached and the service was over, Grandpa helped Pastor Ankrum shake members hands and say 'goodbye' to everyone. He felt that was part of his job being the Sunday School Superintendent. The cat continued following Grandpa around.

After everyone had left the service, Grandpa looked at Millie and asked, "You ready to go, kid?"

"Yes, sir." The cat suddenly went over to the window and jumped out it. "There it goes again, Grandpa."

They walked home talking about the service, how Pastor Ankrum did a good job teaching about creation, and the funny church sign about the cat. Grandpa said he would have to come up with another good one by the end of the week.

When they reached their house, Millie asked, "Grandpa, is it okay if we have some of that apple crisp with ice cream you made for our bedtime snack?"

"Sure thing, buttercup. You really like that, don't ya?"

"Yes. I love the caramel inside. I remember Grandma making it. You would always have her add caramel, even though she didn't like it. She did it just for me."

"Yes. She did, child."

"I sure miss her, Grandpa."

Grandpa opened the fridge to pull out the apple crisp when they heard a scratching at the door. "What in tarnation is that?" Grandpa looked at Millie and she shrugged. "Wait here".

Grandpa went to the door opened it. It was the cat! It apparently wanted inside.

"Well, lookee here, Granddaughter. It's the church cat," said Grandpa. The church cat walked right in and jumped up on the couch. It began cleaning itself. "Makin' yourself at home, are ya? You're a good girl, ain't ya?" He asked, petting the cat.

"Grandpa, how do you know if it's a boy or girl?"

"Most of these black and orange cats are girls. God made all 'em different colors. Boy, I feel the need to use this as another church sign."

"Oh Grandpa. Only you... only you." Millie shook her head.

"Well, it looks like we have a new family member Millie. We can't have a new member without a name. What'cha think a good name will be?"

"How about Claude?"

"Na. It sounds like one of those richy higher-up city folks. I think I have a perfect name. How about Traveler? Since she has been following us everywhere we go."

"I love it!" Millie squealed. "Traveler it is!" She sat on the couch beside Traveler. She no sooner sat down then the phone rang.

"Well, I wonder who that could be at 10 o'clock at night?"

As Grandpa walked over to answer the phone, Traveler jumped up on Millie's lap and started 'playing piano' on her lap. Millie started scratching Traveler's left ear. The cat purred as she listened to the conversation on the phone.

"I see. I see. What in the world happened? Are they okay? Yeah, all the nurses at Camden Clark Hospital are wonderful. I'm glad they got ahold of you, Pastor, and you gave them a ride home. Thanks for letting us know, Pastor. If there's anything we can do, please let us know. Thanks again, Pastor. Bye for now."

Why was the Pastor calling so late?

Grandpa walked back into the living room, saying, "Well, the brother and sister that came to church Sunday were in a bad accident."

Millie gasped. "Is everything okay?

Grandpa went on to explain, "Well, they were on Elizabeth Hill when a deer came running out in front of their vehicle. They hit the deer, and the car spun out of control over onto an embankment. They are okay. Pastor gave them a ride home and just wanted to let us know why they weren't in service tonight as they had promised." Grandpa looked at Traveler. "Boy, Millie, Traveler is definitely playing piano on your leg. "Unclouded Day,"" I think.

"Either that or "I'll Fly Away,"" Millie said with a giggle.

"Be fishers of men- not keepers of the aquarium that cats love to stare at," The next church sign said.

Revival continued until Saturday night. Saturdays usually drew more of the lawn crowd as people didn't need to worry about getting up for work the next morning. Pastor was always appalled by all the beer cans on the lawn Sunday morning. Grandpa would always calm him down and tell him that at least they are being still and not drinking and driving. They were hearing about the Lord, and that was all that mattered.

Traveler continued to be the talk of the town and the church.

She had a big surprise for everyone one Sunday morning, when as she was lying on the top of the church step, nursing 5 kittens. Grandpa found her a cardboard box and a blanket to place in it, then moved her and the kittens inside. The box was beside the piano bench, so she and the little ones wouldn't miss Grandpa's fiddle playing. They never missed out on hearing about the Lord, too.

Jonathan and Monica started making the Owl Hill community their home. Monica finished her teaching assignment and started a new job as an interventional specialist at *Wirt County High School*. She decided to stay with Jonathan in their grandma's old house. Jonathan continued his job working at home as a computer analyst. Working in the country, the Internet became challenging at times. He always managed to figure it out. He also continued to work on his grandma's house, painting and fixing it up.

Aunt Hilda moved in with Grandpa and Millie as her health started declining from her falling and breaking her hip. Jonathan became a Deacon at the Owl Hill Church and started dating Millie. Millie continued helping Grandpa around the house and farm, and helped Aunt Hilda be as comfortable as possible.

Traveler was still the talk of the town as the 'cat who attended church'. She was there every service, and followed Grandpa everywhere around the church. When she wasn't nursing her kittens, of course.

And that, my friends, is the Tale of The Country Cat.

The Fable of the Christmas Spider

MKS Cooper

MANY YEARS AGO, THERE lived a spider whose name was Argiope. She spun her web behind the stove in a house just outside the village called Bethlehem. Argiope earned her place in the household. The family's pie, cooling on the windowsill, and the bread rising on the hearth of the fireplace, were seldom bothered by flies, because Argiope trapped most of them in her web.

One day, Argiope heard the family talking about the visitors they were expecting. Papa was excited. His brother from Galilee would be arriving in a few days with his wife to register for the Emperor's census. But Mama said,

"They will see the dirt on our floor. They will notice the spider webs in the corners. We must get busy and clean our house."

Papa told Mama, "Our visitors are coming to Bethlehem to be counted so they can pay taxes to the Emperor. They are not coming to look behind your stove!"

Mama and her daughters cleaned everything anyhow. They washed floors, polished lamps, and swept Argiope's web out of the corner. Argiope ran as fast as she could, but Mama saw her and caught her in the broom bristles. With a swoosh of the broom, Argiope flew out the door and sailed through the air into the bright morning sunshine. She landed far away from the house. She was homeless.

Picking herself up out of the dusty yard, Argiope set out to look for a new home. She walked all day, peeking through windows and doorways, but it seemed as if all the families in Bethlehem were preparing for visitors. Everywhere she went, Argiope found people sweeping, dusting, and polishing. Family and friends from far away would be arriving soon. Not wanting to get caught in a broom again, Argiope traveled on, growing more convinced with each step that she would have to sleep outside in the cold night air.

Now, after walking so far, daylight was soon gone. Argiope could see the buildings of the village at Bethlehem ahead, lit up by the lanterns that showed here and there in the homes and shops. Gathering what energy she had left, Argiope headed for the lights.

As she came close to the inn at the edge of the village, the strong smell of caravan camels greeted her. Oxen lowed and men called out to one another. Argiope was in a courtyard surrounded by a stone wall. She climbed to the top of the wall to avoid the animals and the crowd of people, who were gathered at the well in the center of the courtyard. Spying a crack in the wall of the inn wide enough for a small spider, Argiope squeezed through and looked around. She was inside the stable!

There was not much light in the stable. Blinking her eyes to adjust to the darkness, a cow came into view. The cow was chewing on her cud, her tail swishing flies off her back, and it reminded Argiope of the flies she caught in her web behind the kitchen stove.

Maybe this would be a good place for my new home, she thought. *After all, who would sweep a spider's web out of a cow's stall?*

Argiope was exhausted. Her eight legs wobbled and she was weak. With great effort, she lifted one tired leg and then another, and then another, until all eight of them carried her the final distance of her long journey into this new place: a cow's stall in the stable of an inn at Bethlehem.

She chose the farthest corner of the stall. Too tired to spin a web, she settled into the sweet-smelling hay and was soon fast asleep.

Was it the hushed voices that woke her? Or was it the bright light that was shining from somewhere outside the stable? She wasn't sure, but one thing Argiope did know-something was happening in the stable.

Creeping to the doorway of the cow's stall, Argiope looked in amazement at the scene before her. The stable was filled with shepherds. They were staring into a manger that had been empty when she arrived at the inn. Now it contained hay, and something else that moved around. A man and a woman stood silently as the shepherds talked quietly among themselves.

Creeping closer, Argiope heard them saying, "It's as the Angel said it would be. Truly this must be the Son of God, the Messiah."

While Argiope lived in the house on the outskirts of Bethlehem, she often heard Papa and Mama speak of this Messiah. He was to be the Savior of the world, God's Son. What did the shepherds see in the manger that made them think it could be Him?

Suddenly, a tiny foot kicked up over the edge of the manger. There it went again, followed by a tiny fist waving around in the air. Then the cry of a newborn infant pierced the quiet of the stable.

Argiope's curiosity overcame her usual shyness at being too close to humans. She skittered across the floor of the stable, and climbed up the side of the manger. There lay a boy-child, a newborn babe, nestled in the hay, freed from his swaddling clothes for a while so his mother could rub him with oil. He sucked on his fist and made funny noises.

Could the shepherds' tale be true? They said a great company of the heavenly host appeared to them in the fields as they watched over their flocks of sheep. They were terrified, but the angels said, "Do not be afraid. We bring you good news. A Savior has been born. Glory to God, and peace on Earth." Then they sent the shepherds to find the newborn King, to praise Him.

Argiope gazed at the babe in awe. How privileged she felt to look upon the Son of God. In humility, and with great effort, Argiope bent all eight of her legs and knelt before her King.

Suddenly, a rough voice called out, "Look! There's a spider near the baby!" A large hand swept across the edge of the manger and Argiope found herself once more flying through the air.

Landing with a *plop*, she burrowed into the warm straw to hide. Didn't these people know she was harmless? Trembling from the shock of being sent flying again, Argiope crawled to the farthest corner of the stall to recover her senses. What should she do now? Where could she go to be safe?

She had listened as the shepherds spoke of the angels' message. She, too, wanted to praise the Savior. But she knew if she came close to him again, she would be killed.

After all, she was just a lowly, dreaded spider, of little worth.

She had heard the baby's mother call him Jesus. Argiope cried out in her heart, *Oh, little Jesus, if you are the Savior, then save me. I only wanted to worship you, but I have no voice. I'm not allowed to even look at you or be near you. I have no way to praise you. I am worthless.*

Argiope's tiny being suddenly filled to overflowing with a warm, unfamiliar feeling. She heard words in her mind- silent, powerful words: *I spoke, and all creation came to be. All things are to praise me- the heavens, the angels, the sun, moon, and stars, the dragons and deeps, fire, hail, snow and wind, mountains, hills and trees, the beasts and all cattle and creeping things, kings of the earth and all people, princes and judges, both young and old men and maidens, and children. Let them praise the name of the Lord, for His name alone is excellent, His glory is above the earth and heaven.*

Dear Argiope, you are not worthless. You have a gift that no other creature has been given. You can praise me by being what I made you to be. I created you, and you are precious to me.

The voice stopped. Argiope was left to think of all that had been said. Creeping things! Even creeping things are to praise Him! *But how?* she wondered. *What was I created for, and what do I have to offer to the King of Kings?*

It was quiet in the stable. The shepherds had gone back to their flocks in the fields. The infant and his mother and father were sleeping. Argiope crept to the wall that surrounded the stable and its courtyard. She looked into the night sky at the bright star that had guided the shepherds to this place.

Still wondering how she could praise God and His Son, she turned to go back to her corner in the stall. The twisted trunk of a large olive tree grew next to the wall, its scraggly branches hanging over into the courtyard. It's bare branches waited for the growing season to fill it with blossoms and fruit.

Argiope thought of the words she had heard. *'Praise Me, and be what I made you to be.'*

I will go where no one will think to brush me away, she thought. *I will do what I was created to do. I will praise the Lord with all that He has created me to be.*

Argiope crept into the highest branches of the olive tree, and worked through the night. At daybreak, finished with her task and more exhausted than she had ever been, she sought shelter in the cow's stall as faint streaks of light appeared in the sky.

The early morning sun slowly appeared over the horizon of Bethlehem, filling the sky with streaks of gold. Rising higher in the sky, the sun cast its glorious brilliance over the Earth below, shining through the olive tree covered with Argiope's finely woven web of silk, making it look as though it was covered with diamonds!

In spite of her exhaustion, Argiope's thoughts had kept her awake.

I have created a thing of beauty as a gift for God's Son. Diamonds for the King of Kings, made from my body with great effort and sacrifice. It will be remembered as the tale told by those who, they say, were here this night, and passed on to those who come after many years later.

Is it true, this tale we tell? We leave you to decide for yourself. But what Argiope knows is true is that the newborn babe in the manger was real and she, a lowly spider, was there that night to offer her gift and worship the King of Kings.

About the Authors

Alexxa Burton

Alexxa has spent most of her life in Ohio when she wasn't busy exploring the planet Miaca. She has recently began dabbling in poetry after a nearly 20-year hiatus.

When she's not writing, she spends her time in the kitchen creating masterpieces of a different type or spending time with her dogs and cat.

Bill Reid

William E. Reid retired from Goodyear Aerospace in 1991 as a tool designer. From 1994-2007 he was a part of the Football Hall of Fame Festival Communications Committee. From 1984-2011 he was the Assistant Chair for the V.I.P Transportation of the Firestone Country Club Gold Tournament. He sold five photographs for the

"Relay for Life" as the Massillon Museum, and had some of his photography printed in the *Akron Life and Leisure* magazine in 2003.

Bill started writing stories in 2018, and 'kicked them around' for a while. They laid dormant for about a year, and after many rewrites, finished them at the end of 2022/beginning of 2023.

A "Real" Golf Story and *The Blood Man* both appeared in book of which there is only one copy, belonging to Bill, titled "Grandpa Bill's Wonderful Stories Volume 1."

Crystal Hoff

Crystal Hoff has a passion for her family, friends, and faith. She grew up in West Salem Ohio, and graduated from Northwestern High School. She has overcome many challenges in her life, including a turbulent home life, and now writes to inspire others.

Dani DeVendra

Dani was an unpublished author up until this project. She grew up in Ohio and lives with her husband and their daughter. She has been passionate about writing since she was twelve but felt uncomfortable publishing her work. Now, she focuses on the stuff that makes her happy, and sharing her writing is one of them.

Dawn E. Dagger

An avid reader and writer for as long as she can remember, Dawn Dagger is a free-spirited author who loves everything fantastical and caffeinated.

Dawn makes art at every opportunity she can. Whether it's making commentary and gaming YouTube videos, teaching herself the piano, or something entirely new, she's always busy with something.

Dawn has several works, including series like *The Chronicles of Salt and Blood*, *The Atlantic Island: Mosaics Trilogy*, and *DARK*.

Donna J. Bunner

Donna grew up in Norton Ohio. Upon graduation, she received 2 associate degrees, one in Executive Secretary the other in Medical Secretary from the University of Akron. Donna developed a love for the special needs community after attending her daughter's classroom activities in the Multihandicapped classroom. Donna has held several hats during her life from being a single parent to being a medical transcriptionist. She has also served in Special Needs Ministries in Stark County.

Today Donna works as a Direct Support Professional serving the Special Needs Community.

Donna enjoys needlepoint with plastic canvas, researching family history, spending time with family, friends, and cats, scrapbooking, Vera Bradley purses, reading Holocaust stories especially *The Diary of Anne Frank*, and attending church. Donna is also part of the Massillon Public Library Adult Writing Group as she hopes to create writings about her Faith and Autism.

Dwight Parrish

Dwight Parrish is a retired customer relations supervisor who always had a passion for writing. He holds a Bachelor's Degree in Finance and a Master's Degree in Business Administration.

In the early stages of retirement, he completed a creative writing course at Malone University.

He enjoys reading, hanging out at the beach, and listening to music. Dwight and his wife Cyndie live in Northeast Ohio. They have (3) children, (7) grandchildren, and (1) great- grandson.

His debut poetry collection, *Sketches of Me*, is a bestseller.

IMA LIVE

IAM Live is all of us, and tells the stories too close to our heart to put our name to.

Jana Day

Traveling has always been a part of Jana Day's adult life. The people, places and experiences influence her view on the world.

Jana has been writing in one form or another her entire life; from poetry in her early years to song lyrics as a young adult, and business articles during her career. Now she enjoys writing for the pure pleasure of escaping into the worlds that exist in her mind.

Lisa A. Beltz

Lisa is an infectious disease immunologist who worked on HIV and its effects on the immune system at the University of Pittsburgh and Johns Hopkins. She is also interested in the interactions between leukemia cells and different anti-oxidants found in plants, particularly green tea. Lisa also studies the effects of environmental contaminants on the immune system, including material from a Superfund site.

She now is working on one of her passions – writing scientific books as well as infectious disease fiction.

Lisa also enjoys cross-stitching, reading, and playing Ken-Ken.

MKS Cooper

MKS Cooper began composing poetry at the age of ten. A number of those early, handwritten poems were preserved by her grandmother and mother. Though old, tattered, and somewhat faded, they are some of her favorite treasures.

As an adult, MKS added short stories and novels to her repertoire. Her new book, *The Mysteries of Tremont Meadow,* is available online. She also has a children's illustrated book, *The Christmas Horse.*

MKS lives in Ohio with her husband. They share a large family of children, grandchildren, and great-grandchildren who are scattered around the country in Ohio, Illinois, Florida, Georgia, and California. In her spare time, she enjoys reading, knitting, crocheting, crossword and jigsaw puzzles, and music.

You can follow MKS Cooper on her website at Cooperbooks72.com.

Okema N. Bassett

Okema N. Bassett lives in Columbus, Ohio by way of Flint, Michigan. Mother of 5 amazing adult children and grandmother to 2 wonderful grandsons. Okema has always had a love of writing and the written word. She has published several newspaper articles, but is looking forward to indulging in writing more fiction. One of her favorite pastimes is traveling and she enjoys experimenting with trying foods from new cultures.

V. Aglow

V. Aglow embodies the connection when residing in the South. With a heart as warm as her sunlit garden, V. has spent a lifetime cultivating joy in the simple pleasures of life.

Born into a world that often rushes past the beauty of stillness, Vanessa discovered her sanctuary within the quiet embrace of writing. As a dedicated personal journalist and writer, she has turned her pages of words into a book. Beyond her writing skills Vanessa true joy lies in making others happy. Whether through her serving or just being a great listener. Gatherings where laughter echoes through her cozy living room, Vanessa has mastered the art of spreading warmth through small, thoughtful gestures.

A pillar of support for her community, V. is often found volunteering at the local a church, sharing her love for the elderly. Her wisdom, gained through the tapestry of experiences, is a beacon for those seeking solace in the quiet corners of life.

The Wilsons is not just a story, but a celebration of V.'s ability to find happiness in the ordinary and create ripples of joy that extend far beyond her peaceful abode. As she gracefully navigates the tapestry of her golden years, V. reminds us that a life filled with quiet joy is a life truly enriched.